THE ENGINEER'S MATE

THE BLUE SOLACE: BOOK FIVE

C.W. GRAY

❋ Created with Vellum

ANCHORS REST SYSTEM, CHARYBDIS
STATION

"Beckie Boo, you can't mean that." Ma's sad face filled his vid-screen.

Beck Brackenstone winced at the sadness in her voice. "Ma, you have to promise me you won't go bothering my mate. We're courting."

Beck's wooing skills were seriously lacking but having Ma poke her nose into it would make things even worse.

"But the Half-Moon folks need me."

Beck bit his lip. His mate led the Half-Moon Guild. The group of assassins had recently moved to Charybdis Station, and they really *could* use some friends.

Poor Ninetta was recuperating from losing part of her leg. She had a lot of healing to do before she could be fitted for a robotic prosthesis. She needed some love and attention.

"Okay, okay. You can go visit Half-Moon, but you can't talk about me to Beol."

She gasped in outrage. "You're my only son. What else would I talk about?"

"Your five daughters? The million kids you've adopted over the years? Pops?"

"Don't you take that tone with me, young man."

"Ma." Beck wasn't proud of the whine in his voice.

She made a face at him. "Fine. I'll do my best to avoid your mate, but I'm still feeding the rest of them. They need me."

Beck knew that was as good as he could hope for. Beck had met his mate a few weeks ago, and ever since then, Ma and Pops had been pestering him about bringing Beol to *officially* meet them. Then there were his sisters and Selene and Hack. Beck almost felt sorry for the poor guy.

"Well, now that we've settled that, are you going to explain your behavior?"

Beck frowned. "Huh?"

Ma narrowed her eyes. "Ever since you moved into your house, you've been hiding something. You don't even let your pa go into your workshop."

Beck yelped and grabbed his tail. "Hiding? There's nothing to hide. Nothing at all."

Ma's eyes softened. "Oh, Beckie Boo. You're a horrible liar."

"I am not." Beck sniffed.

She smiled indulgently. "Of course you're not, baby boy." Her eyes narrowed, and she gave him a hard look. "Now, explain yourself. For months, I go by your house and your door is locked and your drapes pulled. Normally, that wouldn't stop me, but you even locked me out of your security system." She huffed. "Your pa and I both couldn't hack into it."

Beck rolled his eyes. "I need my privacy. That's all."

"Hmm." Ma gave him a considering look. "A few days ago, I saw a woman and a man sneak in the back, Beck. I didn't recognize them, but they looked shifty. Are you in trouble, baby boy? I know you aren't cheating on your mate, so that can't be it."

Oh gods. Beck groaned. "Ma, just don't worry about it, alright? They're just some of my friends."

"Then why did they duck behind a bush when Leti and I walked by?"

"Uh, they're just really shy?"

"Beck."

"Oh no, look at the time. I need to go, Ma. I love you, and I'll see you at the wedding next week."

He turned the vid-screen off when Ma began protesting and buried his face in his hands. What was he going to do? Ma was starting to notice things, and she would tell everyone. Beck hated hiding things from his friends and family.

Dr. Bloop gave a soft woof and wiggled around Beck's feet. His puppy was only a couple of months old, but they had bonded hard. Beck adored him.

"Oh, Bloopy. Ma will figure things out soon. I just know it." He picked the puppy up and buried his face in Bloop's soft fur. "Courting Beol wears my brain out, and this makes it even worse."

Beck hadn't realized how hard courting was. He had been doing his best to build up the courage to ask Beol to be his date for Sebastian's wedding. The problem was, his mouth and his head didn't always match up. So far, all he had accomplished was making an ass of himself.

He had made it as far as the man's house several times, but then Beol would smile at him. After that, Beck's mind left the building, and he became a ridiculous oaf.

Last time he made the attempt, he set the man's couch on fire. Literally.

"Woof."

"You're right, Bloop. I should go over there and just ask him, but I won't bring the welding torch this time."

"Woof."

"I just wanted to show him my new torch. I made it myself."

"Woof."

Beck grabbed his latest gift and Bloop's leash, then headed for the door. "You're being judgy, Dr. Bloop, and it isn't very becoming."

Bloop followed behind him, little tail wagging.

Beck took a second to put the puppy's new outfit on and surveyed him. Bloop wore a Blue Solace vest and a pair of tiny safety goggles that matched the ones Beck wore when he worked on his projects. His small grey horns poked up above his floppy ears.

Beck nodded. "You may be judgy, but you're also my cutie patootie."

They left the house and walked toward the tram, only stopping four times for important sniffing business.

A short ride on the tram took them to the Half-

Moon sector. The Lord Admiral had built an expansive neighborhood for the assassin guild, nestled between the Blue Sector and the governing center of the station. There were several houses, an apartment building, and a large training complex.

Beol lived in the largest house, closest to the training center. Beck knew it hadn't been his first choice, but the guild wanted their Guild Master to have the best, whether he liked it or not.

"Beck."

He turned around at his name and saw Pris walking toward him. She pushed her son, Darya, in a stroller.

Beck grinned wide. "Hi, Pris. How do you like the new crib I made?"

"It's beautiful, Beck. Thank you so much for giving it to us." She nudged him with her shoulder. "Are you going to do it this time?"

He looked back at the house and whined nervously. "Sebastian said to just ask him. He could say no though, and I don't want him to say no."

"You've got this, Beck. I know Guild Master Beol likes you already because he smiles at you. Smiles! He's not a smiling kind of guy, but when you're around, he's so different."

"I set his couch on fire."

Pris fought a grin. "So I heard. Don't let it get to you. Fire visited yesterday and ate all of Beol's food while his guinea pigs rolled around in their balls, knocking things over."

Beck chuckled. "Fire came by without Sebastian?"

Pris smiled fondly. "He feels safe with the Guild

Master. You have no idea how beautiful that is. The last Guild Master wasn't… Well, he just wasn't like Beol."

Her eyes grew wet, and she sniffled. "You'd better get moving. He has an appointment with the Lord Admiral today."

"Thanks, Pris."

She continued her walk, and Beck turned back to the house, gripping his tail. He considered the large, two-story home. It didn't *look* intimidating.

"Woof."

"Stop bossing me around, Bloop."

"Woof."

"Fine." Beck rolled his eyes. "I'll go."

He walked up the steps, and the door opened before he could knock. The sight of the slender, dark man sent excited chills up and down Beck's back.

Beol gave him an awkward smile. "Beck."

Beck blinked at him, mind gone.

"Woof."

"Oh, uh, hi." He thrust his gift towards Beol. "This is for you. Well, it probably is."

Beol nodded, expression serious. "Thank you. Please come in."

Beck walked through the door, and Beol knelt to pat Bloop on the head.

"It's a pleasure to see you again, Dr. Bloop."

Bloop jumped up and licked Beol's chin. The puppy's whole body wiggled.

Beck watched longingly. He wanted to kiss Beol too. Bloop was a lot better at this whole socializing and courting thing than Beck was.

Beol looked up at him. "Would you like a drink?"

Oh gods. He asked that each time, but Beck had never stayed long enough to get that drink. *This time will be different*, Beck thought. It had to be.

Stay calm. Stay calm. Stay calm. "Yes, please."

Beol led him to the kitchen, and Beck sat at the table and looked around. Beol's kitchen, living room, and dining room were open, giving the downstairs area an airy feel.

He felt bad thinking it, but despite the lovely design, Beol's house was a little bland. There wasn't anything personal or warm to be seen, except the gifts Beck had given him.

The colorful metal flowers Beck had made for his mate sat on a table in the living room. The glass string of beads hung in front of one of the windows, and the colorful throw pillows perched on a new couch.

He just moved in, Beck thought and shrugged. He should give the poor man a break. He was just as judgy as Bloop.

The puppy pranced into the kitchen and went straight for the dog bed in the corner. It sat next to a bowl of water and an empty food dish.

"Did you get a dog?"

Beol looked at Bloop. "Oh, no. I just bought a few things so Bloop would be comfortable when you two visited."

He set a cup of hot, black coffee in front of Beck.

"Oh, my favorite." Beck picked it up and sniffed deeply. "Broacian coffee is the tastiest in the galaxy."

Beol gave him a half-smile. "So I've heard, Sparky."

"Sparky?" Beck blushed. He liked the nickname.

Beol shrugged. "Fits you."

"Are you going to open your gift?" Beck started to get excited and let his tail fall from his hand. He hadn't destroyed anything yet, and his surprise was spectacular. Beol would love it.

Today *would* be the day.

Beol picked up the small metal sphere. There were no buttons to push or places to slide open. He ran his hands over it, eyes widening when the object clicked inside.

"How do I open it?"

"It'll recognize your prints only. You just have to slide your finger all the way round it." Beck took a sip of his coffee and hummed in pleasure. Oh, so yummy!

Beol followed his directions, and the sphere quietly split open, revealing the tiny curled figure at the center.

"What..."

The figure unfurled, and an exquisite little fairy looked up at Beol, sleepily blinking her eyes. Her body was a mixture of chrome and bronze colors, and her wings were fine metal webs. Vines of green metal ivy twisted around her body, and roses dotted across her short, metallic blue bob. Her eyes were tiny amethysts.

The fairy stood and slowly rose in the air, fluttering around to peek about the room. She chirped and tittered when she came to Bloop.

The puppy sat up and reached a paw out, trying to pat her.

She giggled and zipped away, flying around the room.

"Beck." Beol watched the fairy in amazement. "I've never seen anything like her. The way she acts… Gods, she almost seems real."

Beck flushed and hid his face. If only Beol knew how real she was.

"I started building her a few months ago. When I met you, I just knew you would like her."

"Is she… Is she mine?"

Beol's wide dark eyes drew Beck in, and he knew he was caught for good. Beol didn't realize how special he was, and it made Beck want to maim whoever had failed him as a kid.

"Yeah. Well, as long as you two suit each other. She makes her own choices, but I knew she'd like you. I made her a pretty house to put up if you want. I left it at home because it's kinda big."

"No one's ever given me something like this. Wolfe gives me gifts now that he can, but this is amazing, Beck. Thank you."

Beck blushed. "Welcome. Wait. Didn't you get presents when you were little? Why couldn't Wolfe get you stuff before?"

Beol sat across from him. "My parents weren't like yours, Beck. Ma comes by with food almost every day, and Pops stops by to talk each time he goes to visit Hay. Your parents are kind and loving."

Beck frowned. He hadn't realized his parents were already spending so much time with Beol.

"Don't frown, Beckie Boo. I really like your parents."

Beck groaned, and his forehead hit the table. "I'm sorry."

Beol watched the fairy with a thoughtful look. "Like I said, my parents weren't like yours."

Beck sat up. "What were they like?"

"My father was cruel and manipulative. Wolfe and I couldn't show one another a speck of affection, or he would use it against us."

Beck growled. Bloop looked up, surprised.

"I think Mom cared for us, as much as she could care for anyone, but she was completely loyal to our father. They were life-mates."

"Ma says finding your mate is a special gift, but I couldn't hurt my own kids."

"That's because you're you." Beol jumped up and refilled Beck's coffee. "Mom wasn't exactly an angel. People loved her, but Wolfe and I knew she would follow orders. She had a way of making you think you were the most important person in the world, all while feeding information to our father. There were no presents, very few hugs, and no softness or love."

Beck trembled, wanting so much to hug his mate.

Beol shrugged. "Anyway, tell me about this little fairy. I can't believe you made her. Well, I can. You're fucking brilliant, but she is absolutely amazing."

Beck huffed. His mate liked to think he was tough, but Beck could see him clear as day. If he didn't think he'd somehow catch something on fire, he'd hug him.

"She's self-sustaining and just needs a little bit of rest each day to recharge. She isn't hooked into any system, like working androids. She doesn't take orders, but she'll try to make you happy. She's kinda like Bloop. She just wants to be your friend, but she has a mind of her own."

The fairy flew back to Beol and landed on his head. She threaded through his hair, her tiny giggles infectious.

Beck grinned, watching them, then took a deep breath. "While I'm here, I've been meaning to ask you something."

"Yes?"

"Would you consider being my date for Sebastian's wedding? There will be fancy hats and cake."

"How could I say no to fancy hats and cake? I'd love to be your date, Sparky."

Beck vibrated with happiness, tail swishing back and forth beside him. "Thank you, Beol. I'll be on my best behavior, and you won't regret it. I won't even bring my torch with me. Well, maybe just a little one for emergencies."

Beol smiled at him, and Beck forgot his name. Oh, that smile.

$\mathcal{A}$ small beep drew Beol's attention, and he scowled down at his communicator. "It looks like the Lord Admiral is early for our meeting."

Beck snorted. "I've never known Fasi Juren to have an *official* meeting at someone's house. Are you sure it's a meeting and not a visit?"

Beol blinked. "Is there a difference?"

Beck stared at him a moment. "You're actually serious. Yes, Beol. There really is."

A knock sounded at the door, and Beol went to answer it. The fairy burrowed under his collar, and Bloop lifted his head, watching them go.

"Did you hear him, Bloop? He's gonna be my date."

Beol couldn't stop his smile when he overheard Beck's soft statement. Damn, his mate was sweet. It felt like all he did was smile when Beck was around. It gave him a headache.

Beol composed himself and opened the door.

The Lord Admiral of Charybdis Station stood on

his doorstep. The large purple Grell grinned at him before shoving past. "I picked up some lunch at Juniper's. Have you been yet? That boy has a way with food."

"I haven't had the chance to try it."

Ma Brackenstone had managed to keep most of Half-Moon fed during the past few weeks. There hadn't been a reason to venture past his guild's neighborhood.

Fasi paused in the doorway when he saw Beck, and a grin stretched across his face. His eyes darted between Beck and Beol.

"Well, hello there, Beck. Did I interrupt something?"

Beck blushed a deep green. "No, sir. We were just talking about Alois and Seb's wedding."

Fasi snorted and grabbed the seat across from Beck, sorting out containers of food. "Finally. I swear, boy, I was afraid I would need to give you a kick in the butt."

Beol refilled Beck's coffee again and settled his hand on Beck's shoulder. "Beck did just fine, thank you. We'll be attending together."

Beol smirked when Beck shivered at his mate's touch, and his tail started swishing again. Beck didn't need any help courting. His shy awkwardness was fucking perfect.

If Beol was being honest with himself, his whole mate was perfect. Beck was huge and muscular; the exact opposite of the men Beol had fucked before.

He had black hair, that was always tousled, and a short black beard. Beck's skin was a light green, and his body was covered in short, dark green hair. Then there was his tail.

Beol's Grell was cute and shy perfection, and he could stare at him all day long.

The fairy peeked her head out of his shirt and chittered at Fasi.

The Lord Admiral's eyes widened. "Who's that, Beol?"

Beol tapped his chin while he thought. "Tinker," he finally said. Despite the harshness of his childhood, there had been a few good spots. "My mother read me an Old-Earth book about fairies once when I was very young. Tinker will suit her perfectly."

Tinker squealed and climbed all the way out of Beol's shirt. She zipped around the table, chittering and twirling as she flew.

"She's beautiful, Beol. Where did you find her? What is she exactly?"

Beck yelped and grabbed his tail.

Beol gave him a look, then shrugged and lied. "She's a toy. I travel a lot and found her in one of the markets I frequent."

Why would Beck want to hide his newest invention? As far as Beol could tell, Beck and Pops were responsible for most of the advances in ship and weapon designs for Charybdis Station. Was it because Tinker was a toy?

"If you ever come across another, please let me know. Rizzie would love one like her."

Beck jumped out of his seat. "Uh, I better get going. I'll let you two get along with your visit."

"You don't have to go on my account, Beck. I brought plenty of food." Fasi's eyes darted back and forth between them again.

Beck gave them a strained smile. "Oh, that's okay. I've got stuff to do."

Fasi's eyes sharpened. "Does it have anything to do with those two shifty strangers Ma told me about?"

Beck froze, tail in his hand and eyes wide. "Huh? What strangers? I don't know what you're talking about."

Fasi arched a brow. "The man and woman that sneak into your house at night. According to everyone in the neighborhood, they're there almost every night."

Beck yelped. "Everyone?"

Fasi gave him a soft look. "You're not very good at secrets, Beck. Apparently, neither are these two strangers. Now, are you in any trouble?"

"Yes, Beck. Are you in any trouble?" Beol narrowed his eyes. His voice was cold and suspicious despite his best efforts to remain emotionless. Why would two people sneak into Beck's house at night? Beck was Beol's mate, damn it.

"We're fine. I mean, I'm fine. They're just a couple of shy friends. Gotta go. Bye."

Beck scooped up Bloop and ran out the door as fast as he could.

Beol watched him go, gut churning. Of course, Beck wasn't what he appeared to be. He wasn't the clumsy sweetheart who brought Beol gifts and smiled shyly. Fate wouldn't give him an honest life-mate.

He turned his hard expression to the Lord Admiral of Charybdis Station.

Fasi looked surprised at Beck's abrupt departure. "Fuck me. He *is* hiding something. I have to admit I was skeptical when Ma called me."

"Two strangers, you said?" Beol's voice was pure frost.

Fasi gave him an alarmed look. "No need for you to worry, Beol. I know Beck, and that man is as steady as a rock. Most likely, he picked up an embarrassing hobby and doesn't want anyone to know."

"Two people visit him every night in secret, and you think he picked up an embarrassing hobby?"

Beol's heart ached at the thought of Beck fucking anyone but him. Damn. He couldn't possibly be this attached already. They had only met a few weeks ago and hadn't had too many full conversations.

Fasi snorted, amused. "Beol, your mate has been saving himself for you since he hit puberty. Two things I can promise you about Beck – firstly, he would never betray his friends or this station, and secondly, he would never betray his mate." Fasi dished up a plate and set it in front of Beol. "Sit down and eat. Don't you worry about Beck."

Beol pursed his lips and shrugged, doing his damnedest to look unconcerned. He would figure out what his mate was up to, then determine if punishment was needed.

He sat and took a bite. "Shall we begin our meeting?"

Fasi sighed. "This isn't a meeting, Beol. I just wanted

to stop by and see how you and your people were doing. Since the Queen attacked Union Station, everyone's been rattled."

Tinker darted closer to Fasi, then zipped away when he looked her way.

"The accommodations far exceed my expectations."

Fasi swallowed his food. "I'm glad you like the neighborhood. There's plenty of room to expand as your guild grows, but we've tried to leave space for a small garden and park if you all are interested."

Beol nodded, taking another bite. Pris and Beck's mother were already planning a community vegetable garden. They had dragged him to the Blue Sector's produce garden to talk to the manager there. He still didn't understand why he was forced to go with them.

"Engineer Hayward appreciates the personal workshop in the training center."

Fasi laughed. "I know Pops and Beck, and they insist on their privacy when working. I'm glad he likes the workshop."

"Beck and Head Engineer Brackenstone are excellent liaisons in adapting our technology. My engineers enjoy their company."

"That's not surprising." Fasi grinned. "Our ships have adapted your shields and quite a bit of your weaponry. Pops and Beck are now working on adapting your personal weapons."

Beol scowled. "Perhaps Dru will give me back my vibro-blade if she was to have her own."

"Yeah, that's not happening." Fasi shook his head.

"I'm not pleased with General Hackett's Weapons

Specialist. She comes by once a day and searches my house. She's already taken several weapons of mine."

Beol knew Beck adored Selene, so he restrained himself from killing the woman. Hopefully, she didn't decide to bring Dru with her next time. She had already taken his personally adapted phaser.

Tinker flew closer and closer to Fasi.

Beol ate another bite. "It's very awkward. Members of my guild were present last time."

Bendix had shown Selene where Beol kept his new favorite vibro-blade.

Fasi was clearly struggling not to laugh. "Selene is… concerned about you being Beck's mate. She'll settle down when she gets to know you."

"I may not have any weapons left by the time that happens."

Fasi snorted, then covered his mouth, composing himself. "I'll be happy to compensate you for anything she takes."

Beol arched a brow. "Hmph. Leti visits far too often too. Every single day, Lord Admiral. He just walks right in and chatters at me for an hour before leaving."

Beol had to admit Leti was kind of growing on him. He'd tried not to like the man since he stole Wolfe, but Leti was too damn loving. Plus, his kids were really entertaining.

Tinker finally grew brave enough and landed on Fasi's shoulder. She pressed her metal hands to his face and chirped, curious.

Fasi smiled and stayed still as the little fairy explored his face. "Leti is just friendly, Beol. Friends are good to have. Anyway, have you given any more thought to my proposal?"

"I'm thinking it over. When I'm ready, I'll bring it up with my guild. We'll decide as a group."

"That's an excellent idea. With a change this big, you'll need everyone on board. Once you decide, I'll bring it up to the Council."

His comm pinged, but he didn't need to look at it to know who was approaching the house. They had seen the Lord Admiral arrive.

"Knock, knock." Noe's voice filtered into the kitchen.

"We're in here, Noe." Fasi smiled cheerfully.

Pris rushed across the living room, hands full of groceries. "We're here to replenish your fridge, Guild Master."

Otto, Noe, and Bendix followed behind her, arms full of more bags of food.

"Where's Darya?" Fasi stood, steadying Tinker on his shoulder.

"Right here." Hay ambled in with the baby in his arms. Beol's brother, Wolfe, walked beside him.

Fasi took the baby, and Tinker darted over to Beol, crawling into his shirt again.

"What was that?" Pris ran over and looked down Beol's shirt.

"Pris!" Otto didn't sound amused with his wife's actions.

"She's so pretty. Come on, sweetie. We won't hurt you."

"What *do* you have down your shirt, boss man?"

Bendix leaned against the counter and smirked. Tinker poked her head out, and Bendix's mouth fell open. "You have a fairy? Seriously?"

"She's beautiful." Hay's voice was full of awe. "I've never seen such craftsmanship."

"I thought you bought her at a market? How do your friends not know about her?" Fasi eyed him suspiciously.

Beol ignored him and coaxed his fairy out so she could meet his friends. "This is Tinker."

The fairy looked around the room and tilted her head. She looked back at Beol with a curious expression. If she weren't made of metal, he would swear she was alive.

"Tinker, this is my brother, Wolfe, and our friends. They're good people, just like the Lord Admiral there."

Fasi preened.

Tinker slowly flew around, landing on each person's shoulder and patting their cheek. When she reached little Darya, she cooed and snuggled against the baby.

"Guild Master, I need one. Please?" Pris's eyes were full of longing. "I really need a fairy."

"Yes, Guild Master," Fasi said dryly. "Maybe you could pick up several when you're next at that *market*."

They stayed, ate, and talked for a while. Before he knew it, the outdoor light was dimming to mimic night time.

"I'd better get home." Fasi stood, stretching. "It was nice to catch up with you all. If you need anything, please let me know. Oh, and I should warn you, Beol.

Beck's family will be at the wedding. Just so you know."

He patted Beol on the shoulder before heading for the door.

Beol ignored Fasi's warning. He could handle Beck's family, damn it. Why did everyone sound so ominous when they mentioned them?

"Otto, are you still good to take the job on Derelict?"

"Yes, sir," Otto said with a grin. "One fucked-up con-artist is on my list. I leave tonight and will be back in a week and a half."

"Moyra wants the contract for the wealthy prick on Siletus," Bendix said. "You know she doesn't take kindly to rapists."

Beol spent some time talking business with his friends before they each headed out for the night until it was just Beol, Hay, and Wolfe.

His brother watched him closely, waiting.

"What do you want from me?"

Wolfe grinned and signed. "Beck came by today."

Beol shrugged, going for nonchalant. Tinker played in his hair, throwing him off.

Hay chuckled. "Did he finally ask you to the wedding?"

"He did. We'll be going together." Beol scowled. "Maybe."

"Maybe?" Wolfe didn't look pleased.

Beol stood and started pacing. It shouldn't bother him that Beck had other lovers. They weren't really a couple.

He stilled and faced his friends. "Two people have been paying him late night visits, and he has kept it all from his friends. I don't think Beck is as innocent and sweet as everyone thinks. It figures, right? Of course, my life-mate would turn out to be duplicitous."

Hay snorted. "Beck? We're talking about Beck here?"

"Yes, we're talking about Beck."

Wolfe gave him a worried look. "He isn't Mom, Beol. I observed them for months. He is exactly what he appears to be."

"Is he?" Beol scowled and headed for the door. "I'll just see about that."

"Where are you going?" Wolfe and Hay followed along behind him.

"I'm going to see what Beck is hiding."

"Son, you need to leave well enough alone." Hay had to jog to keep up with him. "If Beck has a secret, he'll tell you soon. Slow down. My knees aren't what they used to be."

Beol slowed, and they all walked toward the tram. Tinker sat on his head, holding onto his hair.

"Wow, you should see the expression on her face." Wolfe watched the fairy. "It's like she's never been outside."

Hay smiled gently as the fairy chittered excitedly. "Where did she really come from?"

"Beck made her." Beol frowned. "He didn't want the Lord Admiral to know that."

"That's odd." Wolfe looked confused. "Beck has a really good relationship with Fasi."

Beol eyed his brother. "Have you noticed anything odd? You insist on living with Leti, and that's just a few houses down from Beck's home."

Wolfe gave him a look. "I don't spy on my neighbors. However, now that you mention it, Leti did say something about seeing a strange man and woman. He asked Sebastian about it, and he told Leti to mind his own business."

"So, Sebastian likely knows what's going on," Hay mused. "Maybe you could just go ask him instead of spying on your mate like a creep."

"Sebastian is his friend, so he would just lie for him."

"Beol." Hay pulled him to a stop as they reached the shuttle tram. "Please don't do this. Call Beck and ask him to lunch tomorrow. Go to Juniper's and talk to your mate. Give him a chance to share his secrets."

Beol closed his eyes for a moment. "I need him to be the Beck I thought he was."

Hay sighed and tugged him until he started back toward the house. "I loved your mom, I really did, but there are days I despise her for what she did to you boys."

"Beck isn't Mom," Wolfe signed. "I promise."

"I'll try." Beol swallowed hard. "If he doesn't tell me, then I *will* find out. Beck and I won't have secrets between us."

"Alright, son. Now, I know you never learned to dance. Want me to show you some basics for the wedding? From what Pops told me, Beck likes to dance."

———

LATER THAT NIGHT, BEOL SAT ON HIS BACK PORCH. Tinker flew around, stopping to look at each small tree and bush.

Beol waited patiently, and sure enough, a large shifted Grell with a shaggy green coat hopped over the fence.

Beck was much more confident in his canine form. He wiggled his butt and pranced over to Beol, tongue hanging out.

"Hey there, handsome."

Beol held his hand out and stroked Beck's back until his mate settled at his feet, head on his paws.

"You know, you could shift."

Beck looked up and whined.

"You're still nervous, huh? It's alright, Beck. I like you any way I can get you." Beck wasn't the only one who was more confident when he was shifted. "Meet me for lunch at Juniper's tomorrow, alright?"

Beck gave him a happy look and nodded before settling back down.

Beol leaned back and watched the luminous blue shield that surrounded Charybdis Station. He could pick out the six planets that dominated the system and even see Grellweir's largest moon.

He listened to Beck's breathing and let the tension slowly leave his body. Beck had a secret, and Beol would find out what it was. Until then, he'd enjoy every single second he was with his mate.

---

3

*B*eck shut the front door behind him, shuffling Bloop and the small potted plant in his arms so he could lock the door. It wouldn't do for wandering friends to end up in his workshop.

"Are you ready to do this, Dr. Bloop?" Beck held the puppy up. Bloop wore a Charybdis Station lab coat today. Safety goggles perched on top of his head.

"Hey, Beck." Sebastian waved from the sidewalk. Fire stood beside him, shoveling cinnamon candy in his mouth.

"Hey, guys." Beck bounced down the walk. "I'm meeting Beol for lunch. We're having a date!"

Sebastian smiled gently. "That's wonderful."

Fire elbowed Sebastian. "Tell him, Sebby."

Sebastian rolled his eyes, then smiled hesitatingly at Beck. "So, when I'm meditating, my mind wanders over the station. I don't usually pry, but a few days ago, something at your house caught my attention."

Beck paled and squeezed Bloop. "Oh, no. Sebastian, you can't tell anyone. This is bad, really bad."

He started to turn back to the house, but Sebastian grabbed his arm. "Beck, don't worry. We won't tell anyone. Fire already snuck inside yesterday to visit. I thought I'd go by today."

Beck let Sebastian pull him into a hug.

"I understand why you haven't said anything, but you should trust your family and friends. No one will judge you."

"What about Beol? What will he think about me?"

"He's your mate," Sebastian said, smiling. "One day very soon, that scarred man is going to fall in love with you."

"I… I have a date."

"Yes, you do. I'll let myself in and go say hello."

"You'll love them, Sebby. Nice outfit, Dr. Bloop." Fire danced around Beck and pressed Beck's new password into the security panel. The door opened easily. Fire blew him a kiss. "Have fun, Beck."

Sebastian winced. "Sorry about him. If it's any consolation, he can get into every house in the neighborhood."

Beck stroked the scales on Bloop's belly as he hugged him close. "I should go with you."

"No." Sebastian turned him toward the shuttle tram and gave him a shove. "You have a date, Mr. Brilliant Engineer. I promise I'll be nice, so get moving."

"Promise, Sebastian?" Beck was so unsure. He loved his family and friends, but this was so important.

Sebastian patted his shoulder. "I swear, Beck. What

you've done is beyond amazing. I wish you could see them in the spirit world like I do."

Beck took a big breath. "Okay. I'm going to Juniper's. If you need me, I've got my comm."

"Tell Beol I said hi." Sebastian jogged to the front door and disappeared inside.

"Oh, Bloop. This really isn't good."

"Woof."

"You're right. I should just trust everyone. You're a wise dog, Bloop."

A short time later, Beck reached Juniper's Diner. Juniper's chicken, Miss Speckles, perched in her normal flowerpot, people watching. Bloop didn't like it and growled.

"Bloopy, she can people watch if she wants to. You just leave Miss Speckles alone." Beck carried Bloop around to the back of the diner.

Several of their friends had pets, so Juniper had made sure to include a sizable backyard play area for them when he'd designed the diner.

Juniper's pot-bellied pig, Pork Chop, ran around the yard with a few other dogs and one cat.

"Dr. Bloop, there's Pork Chop. Be good for him." Beck set the puppy down and watched him run to the pig, yipping and wagging his tail.

"Beck." Beol's voice came from behind him.

"Hi," Beck said, turning around and blushing. He handed Beol the plant. "I brought you this. It's an aloe plant from Grellweir. Ma says you have to have one in your kitchen if you're gonna have a kitchen."

"Thank you," Beol said solemnly, then handed him a

box. "This may be my first date, but I did remember to bring a gift."

"First date?" What kind of idiots had Beol dealt with all his life? Beck thought the man was made for wooing.

"There was never any time." Beol shrugged. "Come on, Sparky. Let's get some lunch."

"Wait." Beck shot him a look and clutched the box to his chest. "I need to open my gift."

Beol chuckled.

Beck opened the box and smiled. Inside was a simple, black leather bracelet. Silver and blue threads formed a half-moon on the top.

"I love it." He held out his arm and wiggled his wrist. "Put it on, please."

"You really like it?" Beol picked it up and fastened it around Beck's wrist.

"Yep. Don't get much jewelry, and this is perfect. I can wear it while I work."

"I thought you'd like it. Ready for lunch?"

Beck tried not to bounce as he followed Beol into the diner.

"Well, hello," Juniper said. Beck's friend smiled widely and led them to a table in the corner. It was right next to a window overlooking the pet playground. "You're lucky Hack is in meetings all day or he'd be here to stalk you two."

Beck frowned. "I don't know what's wrong with him lately. He hasn't been so grumpy since before meeting Leti."

Juniper gave Beol a pointed look. "Gee, I don't

know. Maybe it's because his sweet gentle giant of a best friend found out his mate leads a group of assassins."

Beck made a face. "That's stupid."

"I agree, sweetness." Juniper patted his shoulder. "You and Beol fit together."

Beol arched a brow. "You can see all that, can you?"

"Darling, you would be amazed at what I can see." He winked at Beck, then headed for the kitchen.

Beck nibbled his lip. What did that wink mean? Was Juniper just teasing or did he know something?

"The Lord Admiral assures me everything here is good. What would you suggest?" Beol's dark eyes distracted Beck from his worry.

"Juniper's a good cook. He makes these tasty Union Station sausages." Beck's smile disappeared. "I forgot for a minute. Union Station's gone."

"It's not gone," Beol said firmly. "There were survivors, and they'll rebuild, just like it has hundreds of times in the past."

"Did you live there long?" Beck knew Beol's guild was based there for years before moving to Charybdis a few months ago. He didn't know how long Beol had been in the guild.

"All my life. Wolfe and I were born and raised there. I've been all over the galaxy, but Union Station was where home was."

"I'm so sorry, Beol." He reached out and took Beol's small hand in his own.

Beol squeezed his hand. "Home is here now, Beck. I wish Union Station was still standing, but there's a reason Wolfe wanted to leave it behind and move here."

"I'm glad he did. I'm glad you and your guild folks are here."

"Are you two ready to order?" Juniper smiled brightly, before frowning at them. "Why the sad faces? You two need a drink?"

Beol snorted. "We're fine, thanks."

They ordered, and Juniper reluctantly left them alone.

"No more sad talk," Beol said briskly. "Tell me what you love most about being an engineer?"

Beck leaned back and grinned. "That will take all year. I always wanted to be an engineer like Pops."

"He's impressive."

"Yeah," Beck said, smiling proudly. "He loves this station."

"Why did you choose Blue Solace? Why be a ship's engineer?"

"Well, I'm not anymore. I mean, Hack leads a fleet now, so he doesn't travel so much and has bigger responsibilities. I guess I chose Blue Solace because of Hack. I love him and wanted to make sure he stayed safe. I like taking care of the ships. It's soothing and gives me time to think up things."

Beol smirked. "I've seen some of those things in action. You're creative."

Beck blushed. "That's what Pops says. He says my head needs to stay in the clouds because good things come from it." He leaned forward, wiggling with excitement. "Leti was reading the kids a story a while back and it made me think. It was this Old-Earth story about a guy named Daedalus. He was an inventor."

Beol smiled softly. "I can see you hiding in your workshop, coming up with all kinds of amazing things.

"I think that's what I like best about being an engineer. There's the practical stuff like Pops handles – building onto the station, maintaining the ships and the bots we use. Then there's the fun stuff. I love playing with the weapons and shields, coming up with new gadgets. I get to protect folks. All that's my job, you know? I love it."

Beck swallowed. He wished he could tell Beol about Becca and Gregor and their secret.

"I'm glad you love your job." Beol looked wistful. "I love my guild, but I'll never be passionate about killing people. Not really. We take out a lot of garbage, but it's a very practical career."

"Well, at least there's money in it. We were mercs for a long time, and there's nothing wrong with getting paid for doing your job. Renee admires you guys a bunch. She said since you've taken over, Half-Moon's become a respectable guild."

Beol started laughing. "Only Renee Juren would call an assassin's guild respectable."

Beck laughed too. "Hey now, *we* were mercenaries a year or so ago."

"Charybdis Station has never been like other mercenary groups."

"Ain't that the truth?" Juniper put their plates in front of them. "Charybdis started as a small group that were more family than business partners. We may have a large population now, but there's still that feeling of family at our core. Then we developed that inconvenient thing called morality. Makes sense that we'd transition."

"Yep. We built good relations and that's paid off." Beck nodded. "Well, some of us made good impressions. Hack never really got that part of things."

Juniper snickered. "Remember when he set that ambassador on fire and wouldn't put him out until his secretary transferred credits into our account?"

Beol looked at them both in surprise. "Seriously? You all seem to set things on fire a lot."

Beck chuckled. "The man was an ass and owed us money for escorting him across two systems. Hack just made sure we got paid. Plus, you know, he's Burnished. They make fire happen a lot."

"Dear cucumber salad," Juniper said. "What is your dog doing?"

They looked out the window.

Bloop and Porkchop chased the cat around the yard. The poor feline moved fast and climbed one of the small fruit trees.

"Poor Potato," Juniper said. "Porkchop gets along with every cat except Remy's. Potato is a sweet kitty, but Porkchop feels like he needs to taunt the poor thing."

"Porkchop is teaching Dr. Bloop bad habits," Beck said, mock frowning.

"Uh oh," Juniper said. "Fluffle just showed up. Shae drops him off sometimes when he gets it into his head the cat needs company during the day."

Selene's extremely fuzzy calico cat stalked toward Bloop and Porkchop.

"Look out, Bloop." Beck covered his mouth and laughed. He loved Fluffle.

Bloop and Porkchop circled Potato's tree, but Fluffle jumped and landed on Porkchop's back. The pig stopped moving, frozen in what Beck could only assume was fear. Bloop wasn't a stupid dog. He took one look at Fluffle and ran the other way.

"Fluffle is such a badass," Beck said, laughing. "Just like Selene."

Beck's laughter died off when he noticed Beol's eyes on him. Beck's mate sat across from him with a soft look on his face.

Beck blushed.

They ate lunch and talked for another couple of hours. Beck couldn't believe he was with his mate. With every story they shared, he learned more and more about Beol.

"You're lying," Beck said, laughing. "Wolfe wouldn't do that to you."

Beck snorted. "He hates getting dirty. He shoved me into that pit to save his clothes, I swear."

"Your target *was* down there," Beck pointed out with a smile.

"Yet, somehow, Wolfe managed to stay clean on solid ground."

Beol's comm chimed and he groaned. "Damn it. I bet that's Bendix. We have paperwork to fill out for the Lord Admiral and a meeting soon."

"Is it hard, making a home here on Charybdis?"

"It's not easy exactly, but it's for the best. My people need a home, and Charybdis needs more protection. You all have managed to piss off some powerful people."

"We." Beck waved between them. "We pissed them off. You're a Charybdis Station citizen now, remember?"

Beol grabbed his hand. "It's worth it. For my people and for me." His comm chimed again, and he sighed. "I guess I should go."

"Look, Bendix." Hack's loud voice cut into Beck and Beol's happy bubble. "I told you he was right here."

The two men stood over the table.

Bendix cleared his throat. "Hey, boss man. We have that meeting with Councilman Warren in a half hour."

"I'll walk you home, Beck." Hack pulled him from his chair and tugged him toward the door.

Beck looked back over his shoulder sadly. "Bye, Beol. I hope your meeting goes well."

Beol watched him go, eyes narrowed.

Once they were out the door, Beck shoved Hack. "I didn't get my goodbye kiss, Hack. That was mean of you."

Hack smiled, unconcerned. "It's not my fault he has places to be."

"I need to get Bloop. Hold on." Beck walked around the diner, then grinned.

Beol stood at the gate, holding Bloop.

Beck gave him a shy look. "We didn't get to kiss goodbye."

"I noticed. I've been looking forward to kissing you,

Beck. I've never kissed anyone before."

Beck's eyes widened in surprise. "Huh? Really?"

"My father would use any weakness against me, Beck. There were only quick fucks with strangers." Beol reached up and cupped Beck's cheek. "I'm glad you'll be my first kiss."

Beck leaned into his touch, liking the way Beol's bare skin felt against his fur. "Not just the first kiss, Beol. All of them."

Beol smiled and nodded in agreement. "All of them."

"I'm a virgin." Beck felt his cheeks flush. He couldn't believe he'd said that.

"What?" Beol blinked. "Really? I thought the Lord Admiral was just a delusional parent."

"Why did he tell you?" Beck made a face. "Never mind. He and Ma are close. I wanted to wait for my mate. I've kissed and stuff, but I've been waiting for you."

Beol slowly smiled, eyes brightening. "I'm okay with that Beck. Very, very okay."

Beck blushed again and looked around. "You really deserve something more special than a kiss behind a diner, Beol."

Beol stood on his tiptoes and pressed his lips to Beck's, giving him a soft, gentle kiss.

Goosebumps covered Beck's arms, even though the kiss wasn't long or deep. They parted and Beol watched him, bemused.

"I think I'm broken. Kissing you broke me."

Beck leaned his forehead against Beol's. "Good. We'll do a lot of kissing. It'll fix you right up."

"Uh, boss man. We really do need to go." Bendix stood a few feet away and gave them an apologetic look.

Hack scowled at them from the street. "Time to go, Beol. Bye now."

"I'm sorry that my best friend's a shithead." Beck kissed Beol again, then walked with him to the street.

"It's alright. Bendix is an asshole too. He's just being nice right now. Wait until you get to know him."

Bendix gasped. "Boss man, did you just imply I'm your best friend? Leti will be mad."

Beol arched a brow. "See what I mean?"

He handed Bloop to Beck.

Beck laughed. "Call me tonight?"

"I will."

Beck watched them go until they turned a corner. He sighed.

"Come on, lover boy. I'll walk you home." Hack wrapped an arm around him. "I'm going to have to get used to him being around, aren't I?"

"Yep."

When he got home, he said goodbye to Hack and ignored his suspicious look. Normally, Beck would have invited Hack in, but that was impossible right now.

Beck went straight to his workshop in the basement. Sebastian and Fire were both still there, and it looked like Becca and Gregor had already arrived. They sat talking with Icarus and the girls.

Beck's son looked up, smiling happily. "Dad, you're back."

4

"Well, what did Beck say?" Hay sat at the kitchen table, eating dinner with Wolfe, Bendix, and Ninetta.

Beol concentrated on his plate and cut his chicken into small, even pieces. Tinker sat on the table beside his plate, watching the movements of his knife.

Wolfe tapped the table and signed. "Beol? What did he say?"

"I forgot to ask." Beol just barely managed not to blush.

"Aww, boss man really enjoyed his date," Ninetta said. She took a bite of her dinner, eyes dancing with laughter.

"I did," he admitted. "I don't want to believe Beck isn't what he seems."

He remembered the press of Beck's lips to his. The warm laughter of the afternoon. Beck wasn't a liar. He wasn't some trickster. He was Beck – sweet, shy, adorable Beck.

"That man doesn't keep secrets well," Hay said. "I asked around, and most of his friends know two folks sneak into his house almost every night. Nettle said the woman's name is Becca. She's a friend of his from college."

Beol sat up straight. "Did she tell him what was going on?"

"Not a thing. Nettle said she distracted him by asking about Lilah and Sophie."

"Juniper knows something," Wolfe signed. "He won't tell me though, and I like him too much to torture it out of him."

"It's evening now," Bendix said, leaning forward.

"I need to know." Beol closed his eyes, feeling sick. "I need to know he's not like Mom."

"Wolfe and I will go with you," Hay said.

Bendix started to protest, but Ninetta cut him off. "I can't go, Bendix. Stay and keep me company. We'll make them tell us when they get back."

"Are you staying the night?" Beol had a room on the ground floor set up for Ninetta. She stayed with Moyra, but sometimes she needed a break from the wild woman.

"If you don't mind, Guild Master."

"It's Beol. Why don't you guys ever just call me Beol?"

"We're working on it, boss man." Bendix started clearing the table. "I'll handle the dishes. You three go be sneaky and find out what's up with your mate. Don't be surprised when the whole guild is here when you get back. We want to know too."

"You could just wait and call Beck tonight, or maybe talk to him tomorrow," Hay said. "Don't fuck up your mating by not trusting him, Beol."

Beol stood, shaking his head. "I need to know."

A short while later, they got off the tram in Beck's neighborhood. Beol activated his shield, going invisible.

Tinker yelped and let go of his hair. She fluttered around above him, agitated and confused.

"I'm still here, Tinker," he said, and she settled down.

"I can't believe we're doing this." Hay activated his shield too, disappearing from sight.

"I should really just go home, but I want to see how fucked up this gets," Wolfe signed, then activated his own shield.

Beol smiled to himself. These two men would always have his back.

He led the way to Beck's home. The small, one-story house sat between Cordelia and Finn's homes. Decorative strings of beads and glass hung on his small front porch and a comfy chair took up the corner.

Tinker flew over to the chair and curled up on it.

Beol deactivated his shield and quickly scanned the house with his comm. He would need to remember to show Beck his advanced communicator. He'd have some fun with it.

"There are three people in the basement, and Bloop is asleep on the couch. Do you two still want to tell me Beck isn't fucking around?" He activated his shield.

It hurt Beol to even say it jokingly.

Wolfe shoved him.

"Come on, son. Let's see you make an ass of yourself." Hay gave him a little shove too.

"Beol, is that you I heard? Are we playing a trick?"

Beol jumped and spun around. Fire stood on Beck's porch, naked. The young Element's dark hair was messy and his eyes full of mischief.

Sebastian's bird, Mustachio, swooped down and settled on the rail of the porch.

Tinker jumped up and squealed. She flew over and landed on Mustachio's back, hugging the bird with her whole body.

"Why are you naked, Fire?" Hay's voice was full of amusement.

"Hi, Mr. Hay. Mustachio and I were flying around the neighborhood. Why are we out here?" Fire felt around in front of him. "Is this Wolfie?"

"Yes." Beol sighed. "We're sneaking, okay?"

"I can be quiet." Fire covered his mouth and mumbled. "See?"

Hay chuckled. "Let's get moving, son."

"Are you Beol's papa?"

Wolfe fell against him, body shaking with silent laughter.

Beol leaned his head back and sighed. "I wish he was, Fire. I wish he was. Now, be quiet and come on."

"Are we going to see Icarus? I spent the afternoon with him."

"Icarus? What?"

Fire opened the door and walked straight to the fridge. "Yummy, yum, yum – BLT time. Hi Dr. Bloop."

Beck's puppy jumped off the couch and followed Fire. He sat sweetly, waiting on his share of the bacon. Fire fed him a full piece.

Hay snickered. "How often do you break into Beck's house?"

"I visit everyone's homes when they're busy. The pets get lonely. So does Icarus and the others."

"Who's this Icarus?"

"Beck's son."

"*What?*"

"Oh dear." Hay sounded concerned.

So much for Beck saving himself for his mate, Beol thought with a scowl. He knew it wasn't fair to be mad since he wasn't exactly virginal himself, but it was the dishonesty of it, he decided. Beck didn't have to put on an act. Beol would have accepted him anyway he could get him.

His heart ached, but fuck, he'd still accept him, even if he wanted an open mating. It would tear him to pieces, but Beol could put up with anything if Beck would just smile at him again.

Over the past few weeks, Beol had felt special for the first time in his life. Today's date just sealed his fucking fate.

They needed to be honest with one another though, he told himself. That was the only way this could work.

Children were a big deal. He had never thought much about kids. He knew he could get pregnant, but his life wasn't suitable for a family. Well, it hadn't been. Now, he *could* have a family, and he would love Beck's son as if he were his own. Once he got past this hurt anyway.

"Let's go." Beol quietly opened the door to the basement workshop and silently made his way down the stairs.

Beck sat at a worktable, tinkering with something, while another fairy slowly buzzed in circles over his head. "He's amazing, Becca. I swear his scent intoxicates me." Beck sniffed and tilted his head. "Gods, I even smell him when he's not around."

A woman laughed. She was in her mid-thirties and Fallon. Her hair was cut short, and her clothes were simple and practical.

"You're hopeless, Beck, but I'm so happy for you."

"Me too, big guy." The man was human and in his early twenties. He had spiked pink hair and blue eyes.

"One day, Gregor, we'll find our mates too." Becca leaned against the man, sighing woefully.

He pushed her away, laughing. "Crazy lady. You'll have to work less hours if you want to meet someone."

"You're one to talk. You never leave the house unless you come here." Beck's voice was full of amusement, though his eyes were focused on his work.

"Where do you think you'll live, Beck? Once you're fully mated."

"I don't know. Beol should be close to his guild. I guess when we mate, Rus and I will move in with him. I'll get Pops to help me set up a good workshop."

"Will he like me, Dad?"

Beol stared at Icarus. He moved around the room,

watering the multitude of plants and humming softly to himself.

He wasn't a child. He wasn't Grell. He wasn't like anything Beol had ever seen. He felt Wolfe's hand on one shoulder and Hay's on the other. He needed the support to remain standing.

Icarus was quite clearly an android but so different than any Beol had ever seen.

The technology behind androids wasn't new. They were used for many jobs that were unsafe or undesirable for sentient beings.

Those creations were nothing compared to Icarus. The android was huge, with muscular arms and long legs. He looked like a mishmash of species – Grell, Betonize, Fallon, and Siren. From what Beol could see, he was a mixture of bronze skin and copper-colored metal.

There was no attempt to make him look completely *real*, but there was also no attempt to make him fit the normal, bland android mold. He was... absolutely unique and amazing.

He didn't have hair, but instead a burnished, black metal design covered the bronze skin of his head. He had dark brown horns and golden Fallon eyes. The tips of his fingers were little claws, like the Betonize.

He looked astounding, but it was his eyes and his facial expression that held Beol's attention. They were intelligent and full of emotion. The android really looked worried Beol wouldn't like him.

He was sentient.

Holy shit! He was *sentient.*

"Of course, he'll like you, Rus." Beck shot a smile over his shoulder. "Once he meets you and gets to know you, he'll love you as much as I do."

"He liked the aloe plant I picked out, didn't he? I know he loved the fairy. Who wouldn't?" Icarus's face was full of joy as he laughed. "He really named her Tinker?"

"He did."

"That's perfect for her. She really wanted to meet him."

"Wasn't that a risk, Beck?" Becca seemed unsure.

"Yeah, but she wanted to be his friend. She needed her own person, just like Dr. Bloop. Hack didn't want to give his grandpuppies away, but he knew it was best for them. Tinker needs Beol." He pointed his compact welding torch toward the buzzing fairy. "This one will pick her person soon too." Beck turned around in his stool and nibbled his lip. "That reminds me though. We need to talk. I've been putting it off, but Ma and the others in the neighborhood have noticed you two coming and going. They're starting to get suspicious."

"Damn." Gregor's shoulders slumped. "Sebastian and Fire were okay with things, but can't you just tell everyone else we're your lovers or something?"

"He just met his mate, Gregor." Becca smacked his shoulder.

"Seriously, Dad. That would make him look like a jerk." The voice in the corner belonged to another android.

She sat with her feet propped up on a long couch. She strummed a guitar while another android swayed to the music.

The musician was pure seduction, from her throaty voice to her golden skin. She had short red hair that framed her heart-shaped face, and rose gold, metallic flowers trailed down one side of her face and along one bare shoulder. Her eyes were similar to Icarus's golden Fallon eyes, but somehow also entirely different.

This android was just as sentient, but she had a hard practicality in her eyes.

Gregor smiled fondly at the android. "You're right, Sax. I wasn't thinking."

"What about telling them you all are friends or are in a club or something?" The dancing android didn't stop her movements but did turn to face the room.

She was full-figured and sturdy, with an honest and open face. She had blue hair cut in a sharp, fashionable style. Her clothes matched her hair – tasteful and trendy.

Unlike the others, her hands and arms were fully metallic. The rest of her appeared to be a mix of white skin and titanium-colored metal.

"Meggie's right. Why don't you just tell them we're friends?" Becca blew the dancing android a kiss.

Beck pressed his hands to his cheeks. "I did that, but they already know something's up, and I can't lie for shit. Do you think Beol will hate me when he finds out I'm hiding our three babies down here?"

While he was still invisible, Beol let himself grin

with relief. Beck had a secret, a huge one, but he was still the Beck that Beol had started falling for.

Beol took a deep breath and turned his shield off. "I won't hate you, Beck."

5

*B*eck gulped when Beol appeared suddenly, obviously deactivating a shield. Hay and Wolfe appeared behind him, both looking sheepish.

"Beol?" Beck nibbled his lip. His mate looked both grumpy and relieved at the same time.

Beck's mate gave him a strained smile before turning to Icarus. "Hello, Icarus. I'm Beol."

Icarus hopped up and rushed over. "You're Dad's mate, right? He's so tiny, Dad." The large android hugged Beol, lifting him off his feet.

Beol's squished face scowled. "You're warm and I hear a steady heartbeat. Gods, Beck."

"He's like a grumpy little kitty, Dad."

Beck snickered. "Icarus, put him down."

Icarus settled Beol on his feet and smiled sheepishly. "Sorry about that."

Wolfe shoved Beol out of the way and held out his arms expectantly.

Icarus grinned and hugged Wolfe too. "You're

Wolfe, right, and you're Hayward? Fire told us about everyone he knew a couple of weeks ago."

"Fire told you a *couple of weeks ago*? I thought he just found out about you all a few days ago?" Beck stood, crossed his arms, and gave him a stern look.

"Icarus, you big mouth." Meggie sent a nervous look Becca's way.

Becca and Gregor stood and echoed Beck's stance.

"What's going on, you three?" Becca gave the three androids a pointed look. "Start talking."

"Hey guys." Fire walked down the steps with Bloop.

Mustachio flew in with Tinker on his back. The little fairy squealed with delight as they flew around the room.

"Fire, why are you back?" Beck gave all his uninvited guests a look. "What are you *all* doing here?"

"What? I can't visit?" Fire looked affronted.

Beck closed his eyes and sighed. "Sax, you're the reasonable one. Please explain."

Sax put her guitar down and leaned back, arms crossed. "Fire showed up three weeks ago today and started raiding your fridge. Icarus went to chase him off but ended up bringing him down here."

"Sax almost cut my head off." Fire wrapped a hand around his throat and glared at the android.

"I thought you were an intruder." She shrugged, unconcerned. "Anyway, he's been back to visit exactly seven times since then."

"He brought his guinea pigs yesterday." Meggie gave Becca an apologetic look. "They're really cute."

Icarus wrapped an arm around Fire's shoulders and

puffed his chest out. "He's our friend, Dad. You said friends are important and can even become family. Fire and Juniper can be my Selene and Hack."

Beck's expression softened. "Oh, sweetie. I do love you." His son had such a big heart. "Wait. Juniper?"

"About a month ago, Juniper came by," Sax said. "Icarus also let him inside. I didn't try to kill him though. He identified himself right away."

"Icarus!" *That explains Juniper's knowing look earlier,* Beck thought.

"You told me he was your friend and could cook really well!" Icarus hurriedly moved to stand behind Beol. "He taught me some of his favorite recipes, and I put them in my box."

Gregor cleared his throat. "What about you three?" He gestured to Beol and his friends.

"Yes, Beol. Why *are* we here?" Hay gave him an innocent look. Beol blushed. Hay cackled. "Holy fuck monkeys, Wolfe. Look at that. He's blushing."

Wolfe grinned at Beol, silently laughing.

Beol scowled at his brother. "Fucker.'

"Fuck monkeys." Sax savored the words. "I like it."

"Beol?" Beck nibbled his lip and clutched his tail.

His mate looked constipated. "I wanted to find out who these two were." Beol winced. "I might have been… Oh, never mind."

"He was jealous," Wolfe signed. "And a suspicious creep."

It was Beck's turn to blush. "Oh. Well, there's nothing to be jealous of. Gregor and Becca are just friends."

"Suspicious creep, huh?" Gregor gave him a pointed look. "Becca and I both know sign language. Your friend's words worry me."

Wolfe smiled serenely. "I'm his brother."

"Oh, give the man a break." Becca poked her friend. "They just met, and they're mates."

"Excellent point." Hay clapped to get their attention. "Now that's settled, will you tell us about your son and his friends?"

Beck went and took Beol's hand, pulling him across the room to a stool. He really needed better seating down here. His mate deserved better than a hard stool or an old chair.

Beck took a breath, then started his explanation. "The three of us met at a bar and got drunk."

"That's promising," Hay said wryly.

Gregor snorted. "We started talking about crazy things, and one thing led to another."

Beol's growl sent a shiver down Beck's back. Fuck a duck, his mate was so sexy.

Becca shoved Gregor. "By that, he means we started planning how to make sentient androids. I'm a neurologist, and Gregor works in the robotics division of medical."

"That's not your normal bar hookup story." Hay looked at the three in amusement.

Gregor laughed. "It *has* led to sneaking around and keeping a deep, dark secret."

"It also led to three children." Becca smiled.

"We aren't kids, Mom." Meggie stomped her foot, and Beck hid his smile.

"I know, Meggie, but you're my baby girl, and I love you." Becca moved to the android and wrapped her arms around her.

Meggie laid her head on Becca's shoulder. "Yeah, okay. Love you too."

"Each one of us planned out our ideal android." Beck continued. "I don't think any of us really thought we would be successful."

"I've never heard of anyone even trying this." Hay shrugged. "Most folks don't want sentient androids. They just want workable, controllable androids."

"That's stupid." Fire set Bloop down and started wandering around the room, poking at things.

Beck watched him carefully before getting distracted by Tinker. The fairy flew from Mustachio's back and landed on Beol's head. She stretched out, lying flat, and started trilling like Mustachio.

Damn it. Beck had a feeling Fire wasn't the only guest to previously visit his house while he was gone.

"We just wanted to create something special." Becca squeezed her daughter. "All of us have a great appreciation for beauty and life. We pooled our knowledge together and made our children."

"Why keep them down here?" Wolfe looked around the workshop curiously.

Beck loved his workshop. The room was large and covered in his gadgets and half-built projects. There were several well-maintained plants hanging around the room and plenty of drab, but comfy, chairs and couches. It was still a basement though.

"When we realized what we had accomplished,

we also realized how they could be abused," Gregor said. Beck's friend went to sit next to Sax. "Androids don't have natural rights like every other sentient species. What if someone stole my Sax and tried to hurt her?"

"I would kill them, then find my way home." Sax blinked, then went back to strumming her guitar.

Gregor grinned proudly. "We created her to be the perfect musician, but damn if she doesn't want to be a soldier. She's good too. Any captain would be lucky to have her on their crew."

Fire gasped and clapped. "We can ask Dru. She's really smart, so she'll see how great Sax is."

"Hold on there, buddy." Becca raised her brow. "Without rights, we're scared they'll be confiscated or kidnapped."

"People will just see them as property." Beck's lip trembled.

Beol growled again, then narrowed his eyes. "Not happening. Icarus, Meggie, and Sax are under my protection. I may not be able to grant them rights as a citizen, but I can damn well make sure no one hurts them."

"You would do that?" Beck knew he had to look like an adoring puppy, but damn it, Beol was his hero.

His mate sighed. "Of course, I would."

Wolfe came to stand behind his brother and dropped a kiss to the top of his head, barely missing Tinker. The fairy squawked and sat up, shaking her fist at Wolfe.

Hay smiled at the two brothers, then looked

thoughtful. "Do you really think the Lord Admiral would hurt them?"

Beck shook his head. "No, but the Council has a lot of influence. What if they want to use Icarus? I created him to be the perfect soldier. What if they think he's expendable because he was created, not born? What if they just see him as a weapon?"

Icarus hopped from foot to foot and hummed nervously. "Dad, you worry too much. I may like cooking better than fighting, but that doesn't mean I can't protect us. Wouldn't it be worth me being a soldier if it meant we could be free?"

Beck could definitely see him as a soldier. The android looked like a formidable opponent, at least until you looked in his eyes. Icarus had a soft heart.

"He wants to be a cook and gardener like Juniper." Beck waved around the room. "Look at all the plants he keeps. I swear, I look at them and they wilt. He knows all Ma's recipes and apparently some of Juniper's. His roast is the best, just, uh, don't tell Ma I said that."

Icarus preened at his father's praise, then gestured to one large, well-kept fern. "That's my fern, Fawn. Isn't she a beauty?"

Beck felt so much love for his son. Damn if Icarus wasn't special, and he would do anything to keep him that way.

"Icarus is Icarus, not some dream soldier. He isn't just a weapon." Beol's voice was soft. "No one should ever be forced to hurt others."

Wolfe hugged his brother from behind and buried his face against Beol's neck.

"Beol?" Beck knelt in front of him, full of worry. "What's wrong?"

"Our former Guild Master was their father." Hay's voice was gruff. "That fucker was a monster. Once he hooked you in the guild, you never left. He would hold your loved ones hostage unless you did exactly what he wanted."

"He was cruel and enjoyed his power." Beol's voice hardened. "I was raised to be an assassin and never had a choice. Hay and I tried to save Wolfe from it, but Father forced him to train and kill too."

Wolfe looked up, eyes full of agony, and signed. "After Mom died, I tried to resist. In punishment, he forced Beol to cut into my throat. He said he would kill me if Beol didn't do it."

"It was the worst moment of my life," Beol said. "I had to hurt him to save him, and now he can't speak because of me."

Beck hugged Beol's legs and his voice trembled. "Why would he do that? Why would he hurt you both that way?"

"To show them who was in control." Hay sat with a groan.

"Those bastards." Becca trembled with fury, and Gregor looked like he was going to be sick.

"I would do anything to keep Beol from hurting." Wolfe looked at Beck. "I do mean anything."

Beck should have been scared, but he was just happy that Beol had someone looking out for him.

"Wolfe." Beol rolled his eyes. "Stop trying to intimidate my mate."

Hay smiled sadly and wiped his eyes. "Anyway, we understand your worry about Icarus. As long as we're around, Icarus won't have to do a single thing he doesn't wanna do."

Icarus rushed over and hugged the old man. "Thank you, Hay. I'll bake you some cookies, okay? What's your favorite?"

"Maybe we should talk to the Lord Admiral." Becca looked hopeful. "If we have your mate's guild behind us as security, it would leash the Council."

"If we're free, I could go shopping." Meggie's eyes grew wide. "I'll be the most fashionable doctor on Charybdis Station."

Beck watched Beol as his friends and their androids chattered excitedly. He sat at Beol's feet, hugging his legs, while his tail swayed back and forth on the floor.

Bloop trotted over and crawled in his lap, settling down for a nap.

"Beol? Your father's dead, right?" If ever a man deserved to die, it was him. Beck hadn't liked his father even before he knew he was the Guild Master everyone hated.

"Yes." Beol hesitated a moment. "When Otto and Pris found out they were having a baby, I knew something had to be done. My father would have used Darya. He would have taken him and raised him to be just like me and Wolfe. That's why no one in the guild dared to have a family. When Otto met Pris, it threw everyone off. Pris isn't an assassin, but Otto fell hard. They're life-mates."

"Wouldn't Otto and Pris fight him over Darya?"

"They would, but my father was the best. He would either have killed them straight out or killed Darya before killing them."

"I'm glad he's dead. Ma always says you should be kind and respect others. If you're not doing that, then you're not fit for living."

Beol smiled and stroked Beck's hair. Beck shivered at his touch.

"When Otto told me Pris was pregnant, I killed my father."

"Oh, Beol." Beck kissed his knee. "That couldn't have been easy."

Beol's laugh was hoarse. "It really was. He thought I was completely under his control, so he didn't see me as a threat."

"I didn't mean the killing part. I meant killing your *father*."

"Beck, he was never a father to me. He may have contributed to making me, but the man was a monster. It really was easy. I wish I had done it sooner."

"I'll share Ma and Pops with you." Beck smiled up at him. "They want to meet you anyway."

"I'll be your papa, Beol." Fire hopped around him excitedly. "I've always wanted a baby. It's a big responsibility, but I can handle it."

Beck started laughing, and the others joined in. He hadn't realized they were listening to him and Beol talk.

Hay chortled. "I'm sorry, Fire, but if anyone gets to be Beol's papa, it's me. I practically am anyway. I sure as shit changed enough of his diapers when he was a baby."

Fire slumped. "I guess I still have the guinea pigs."

"What would Sebastian say to you dragging someone home?" Wolfe's eyes danced with mischief.

Fire stomped and crossed his arms. "He wouldn't even notice. All he does is talk to his new apprentice."

Beck turned around to watch Fire. "Apprentice? What are you talking about?"

"Remy asked Sebby to train him to be a shaman last week. Now Sebastian and Death are busy all the time."

"Is that why you've been visiting me?" Beol cocked his head and considered the young man.

Fire's lip trembled, but he shrugged. "I get lonely."

"Fire? Where are you?" Sebastian's voice came from the top of the stairs.

Gregor snorted. "Gods, your house is busy tonight, Beck."

Becca sighed. "He's down here, Sebastian."

Sebastian stomped down the stairs. "Fire, you were supposed to let Beck and his friends have some alone time."

Fire pouted. "Beol was here too."

"You're a nosy sneak."

"Hey!" Fire looked offended for a second, then laughed. "Did you miss me?"

Sebastian laughed and pulled him into a hug. "Of course, I did. I've gotten used to you being around and don't know what to do when you're gone."

Beck hid his smile. Fire didn't have to worry about losing Sebastian's love and friendship.

The shaman looked at Beck. "What you and your friends have done is magnificent, Beck. Icarus, Meggie, and Sax are as alive and feeling as you or me. They're sweethearts too."

"I am *not* sweet." Sax scowled.

"I see your threads, Sax. You're so sweet it's ridiculous."

Beck ignored her annoyed cursing and flushed with pleasure. He hugged Beol's legs again.

"So, I hear you have an apprentice," Becca said politely.

"Fire!"

"He's a loudmouth like Icarus," Meggie said, shrugging. "It's only fair we know your secret since you know ours."

"We're telling everyone after the wedding," Sebastian mumbled.

Beol looked at Beck, Gregor, and Becca. "We'll tell the Lord Admiral about Icarus, Meggie, and Sax after the wedding too. I'll come with you and give you my full support."

Beck hugged his legs tighter. He couldn't fuck this up.

6

————————

Beol straightened his suit jacket and knocked on Beck's door. Now that he knew Beck's secret, it was time to step up and do his own courting.

He had remembered the customary courting gift but had decided a house plant would work in lieu of flowers. Icarus would help Beck keep it alive, and it would last much longer.

Tinker sat on the brim of Beol's black top hat. She shrieked a hello when Beck opened the door, and Beol almost shrieked too. Damn, but Beck cleaned up well, even if he looked a little odd.

Usually, the engineer dressed in plain clothes that were often smudged with whatever he was working with. Today though, he wore a well-cut, deep purple suit with navy stripes. An old-fashioned, purple bowler hat perched on his head, and a delicate pink rose was pinned to his collar. He was very… colorful.

"Isn't this the best suit ever?" Beck spun around with a grin. "It's brand new."

"You look great." Beol cleared his throat and tried to think pure thoughts. *Damn it.* Why did Beck have to be so large and muscular? Why did he have to be so damn sweet?

"I brought this for you and Icarus." He thrust the plant into Beck's hands.

"Oh, he'll love it! It's awful pretty. Thanks, Beol."

Beck held the plant to his chest and swayed happily while his gaze traveled up and down Beol. They were such a dark green they looked black.

"Hmm, you look yummy. Oh, wait. Icarus picked out a boutonnière for you."

Beck ran back into the house, and Dr. Bloop came to the door. Bloop was dressed in a blue and white tux with his own top hat. A large, grey mustache balanced on the top of his nose. What the hell?

Beck called out from inside the house. "I almost forgot. Did you bring your mustache?"

Beol shook his head. "Huh?"

"Your mustache? It was part of the dress code."

"They were serious about that?"

Beck came to the door and held up a black, droopy strip of hair. "Of course, they were." He stuck it on his top lip, then smoothed it out.

"Unfortunately, I didn't bring one." Beol couldn't force himself to sound sad.

"Hold on. I have an extra."

He ran back into the house, then came back out a few minutes later. He smoothed a black mustache to the top of Beol's lip and pinned a pink rosebud to Beol's collar.

"Icarus said pink roses mean love and appreciation." Beck blushed and shut the door behind him. "Are you ready? Oh, hi, Wolfe. Hi, Ninetta."

The two walked to the house from the street, Ninetta using her crutch and Wolfe watching her closely. Neither one was dressed for the wedding.

"We thought Icarus and the others might like some company," Wolfe signed. "Ninetta wants to meet them and keeps complaining about being bored."

"I would really like to meet them, Beck. Please?" Ninetta batted her eyes at Beck.

"Aww, that's great, guys. Gregor and Becca are down there, but the kids get tired of just seeing us. I know Rus would love more folks to cook for."

"Perfect. This gives me a good reason to avoid the wedding." Wolfe grinned and slipped past them, slapping Beol's butt on the way.

Ninetta snickered as she followed.

Beol snarled after them, then cleared his face. He took Bloop's leash, smiled at Beck, and held his arm out. Beck took it with a shy smile of his own, and together, they walked toward the tram.

"Beol." Hack stood in front of his home. His arms were crossed, and he glared at Beol. The baby strapped to his chest and the children and animals running around him made his glare seem slightly ridiculous. Then there was the large, bushy mustache.

"General Hackett." Beol nodded.

"Everyone settle down and act civilized." Leti Hackett left the house and stalked toward his family. His suit was even stranger than Beck's. It was forest green and the lapel of his coat was covered in tiny, white llamas. His top hat was also forest green, but small, stuffed llamas nestled in the brim. A long, red mustache twitched on his lip.

"Sami, don't chew on Rizzie's dress. Maia, please grab Pepper before she squats in that bush. I'd rather change her diaper than have her shit in the front yard. Grampa Moses, please stand between Rose and Alex, since our two eldest can't seem to behave. Hack, stop glaring at Beol. Mo, put Abbot, Gravy, and Pax back in the house. No pets allowed."

Beol fought the urge to stand up straighter and apologize. Leti may have stolen his brother from him, but he was a force to be reckoned with.

"Dr. Bloop gets to go." Mo pointed toward Beck's puppy. "And what about Princess Buttercup?"

Leti's Fire Veil Dragon stretched along Leti's shoulders and looked bored. Leti arched a brow. "Dr. Bloop is a scientist and Princess Buttercup is royalty."

Mo snickered. "You just want our arms empty in case we need to grab a baby."

Leti nodded, face serious. His mustache twitched again. "You are completely correct."

"Daddy, Sami stole my hat." Rizzie stomped her foot and glared at her little brother.

Beck tugged on his hand. "Uh, we'll see you guys there. Hurry, Beol. Run before Leti yells again."

Hack's glare didn't falter as they ran away.

"I love you, Beol," Leti called from behind them. "Beck, your suit looks wonderful!"

"I like your llamas," Beck called back, then picked up the pace when Leti started lecturing the kids again.

They made it to the shuttle tram and shot off toward one of Charybdis Station's large, central gardens.

"Thank you for coming with me." Beck smiled shyly. "Weddings are fun, but they always make me nervous."

"Nervous?"

"Yeah. Weddings remind Ma and my sisters that I'm single, and they start trying to set me up with everyone they know. Luckily, Selene and a few of the others are still single too. I usually throw them to my sisters and run."

Beol's laugh sounded rusty. "So brave."

"Wait until you meet them. Pops made them promise to leave us alone today, but they'll pin you down soon enough."

Beol grabbed Beck's hand and kissed it. "You aren't single anymore, right?"

Beck blushed and his tail waved behind him. "No, I'm not." He gave Beol a shy look. "Can I… Oh, never mind."

"What is it?"

Beck made a face. "It would probably just annoy you."

"Tell me, Beck." If there was something he could do to make Beck happy, then he'd fucking do it.

"Will you hold my hand today?"

Beol took Beck's hand. "Anytime you want to hold my hand, Sparky, feel free."

Beck smiled sweetly. "I usually just hold my tail when I'm nervous. This is a whole lot better."

Beol brought Beck's hand up for another kiss. "Did you bring your torch?"

Beck nodded and pulled a small cylinder object out of his jacket pocket. He held it up and an intense white fire came from the tip. It looked like Beck had been playing with Half-Moon's flame technology.

Beol snorted. "Put that away. Gods, you're as bad as Hay."

Beck puffed up, proud. "I made it myself. Do you want it? It comes in real handy when I'm working on the ship."

"That means it's perfect for you." Beol shook his head. Damn, his mate was adorable.

They arrived at the garden with several other mustachioed people. Beol recognized a few of Beck's friends and his own guild members, but there were a lot of strangers.

The garden had been transformed into a formal, Old-Earth wedding venue. The reception area was to the left, tucked behind some flowering trees.

"Oh, look, Beol. There's the King of Grellweir and his daughter. I think that's the Queen of Siren's Lament too."

Beol surveyed the guests. "I see all the leaders of Anchor's Rest are here."

"Even Bowan. He's the Chief of Burnished Outpost." Beck waved enthusiastically at a Burnished man standing with the Prime Minister of Fallow. "He's a real good guy."

"I didn't realize Alois and Sebastian were so high profile."

"It's because they're close to Fasi, and Sebastian's a shaman. People are curious. Oh, fuckity, fuck, fuck."

Beck pulled Beol behind a large flower display. "I saw one of my sisters."

"Are they really that bad?"

"You'll see soon enough. I'm supposed to ask you to our weekly family dinner next week. It's going to be at Ma's house this time. They like to alternate."

"I would be honored," Beol said hoarsely.

Why did he feel so light? So happy? He knew he was just standing next to Beck behind a flower display, but being around Beck was like soaking in the warmth of a sunny day.

"Beol." Selene's dry monotone came from behind them, cutting into his happy moment.

They spun around, and Beol snorted. The Siren wore an elegant, dark blue gown and a black pillbox hat. She also had a big bushy mustache.

Her young son Xu stood beside her, glaring at him. Gods, even the younger generation hated him.

Beck chuckled. "Selene, I think only the men had to wear mustaches."

"That's sexist." She stroked the mustache. "I like it."

Xu took a break from glaring and smiled at Selene. "You pull it off well, Mom."

"Thank you." Selene stared blankly at Beck. "Ma called me. You have a secret."

Beck squeaked nervously, and Beol took his hand, squeezing it. "He does have a secret, but we'll be addressing it in two days. We're meeting with the Lord Admiral and the Council."

Selene's expression didn't change, and her voice remained a dry monotone. "You will tell me. Now."

Beck's big dark eyes pleaded with her. "It's complicated."

An usher came to stand with them. "Can I show you to your seats?"

"Yes, please." Beol pulled his mate away from Selene.

She followed behind them as they approached their seats near the front. "I'll wait, Beck, but I'm going with you to see the Council."

"The Council? Why is Beck going to see the Council?"

Beol sighed. Of course, their seats were right next to Hack and his family. Leti was with Sebastian. Wyatt, Leti, and Fire were Sebastian's groomsmen while Sai, Salla, and Cordelia were Alois's groomswomen.

Hack and the rest of his bunch took up two rows.

"Well? Why is Beck going to see the Council? What did you do, Beol?" Hack's mustache looked like it was about to fall off.

Beck groaned, then spoke in a harsh whisper. "For the love of finicky reactors, I helped two friends create sentient androids and am going to inform the Council about our babies in two days. Beol had nothing to do with it."

Hack's mouth hung open, but at least he wasn't glaring at Beol.

"Babies?" Selene tilted her head and watched Beck.

Beck's big plain face brightened with joy. "Icarus is my son. I designed him and created him. I modeled him after you, Selene. He was meant to be a soldier, but he has dreams of his own."

Selene blinked. "You modeled him after me? I'm a mother again." She turned to her son. "Xu, you have a brother."

Xu shrugged. "Okay. Well, as long as I don't have to share a room with him."

Beol scowled. Icarus was *his* future son. "Wait a minute."

"Too late, assassin. You can be his stepfather." Selene tilted her head again. "Perhaps."

"You made sentient androids?" Hack's voice was garbled.

"I'm actually still making them," Beck said in a small voice. He darted a look toward Beol's hat where Tinker was hiding.

"Tinker? She's sentient?"

Beck's smile was strained. "Surprised?"

Before Beol could reassure him, the orchestra began playing the entry music. Beol settled for squeezing his hand and hoped Beck knew Beol wasn't mad at him.

Alois's groomswomen came down the aisle first. Each was dressed in a different color – blue, red, and green – and wore cute pillbox hats with veils.

Beol finally noticed every single person at the wedding wore a hat. All the men sported their mustaches too. Beol almost laughed when he saw Bendix's bushy blue mustache. It matched his hair perfectly.

They all stood when the music changed, and Pops began to walk Alois down the aisle. Alois looked uncomfortable in his white suit and kept pulling at the high collar.

As they passed Beol, Pops gave him a wink.

Sebastian's groomsmen came next, Leti in the lead. Fire waved energetically at everyone as he followed, and Wyatt came in last.

Sebastian's bird, Mustachio, flew low along the aisle, trilling a song before settling on a perch near the front.

Finally, Fasi started down the aisle with Sebastian. The shaman wore a suit similar in design to Alois as well as a big, happy grin. Tears streamed down Sebastian's face, and there was no doubt they were tears of joy.

Those tears are worth wearing this stupid mustache, Beol thought. Sebastian might not be a close friend, but he was a really good person.

Beol leaned up and whispered to Beck. "If you were to marry, would it be a large wedding?"

Beck leaned close. "Big? Yes. Fancy? Hell no."

"No top hats?"

"Nope. Maybe the mustaches though."

Beol leaned back in his seat and smiled. He kissed Beck's hand and watched the formal, Old-Earth ceremony.

There was something peaceful about sitting next to Beck and knowing the man was his. Beol felt a wild and frightened part of himself settle, and he knew he would never again be the man he was before stepping off that ship and spotting Beck.

After Sebastian and Alois exchanged their vows, Selene's sister and brother stepped forward to sing a song as the couple lit unity candles.

Beck stifled a yawn, and Beol gave him a fond look. Weddings weren't exactly entertaining.

Any possible boredom the guests felt fled when the Sirens began singing. Their song was a beautiful ebb and flow of emotions – love, joy, passion, happiness, and peace. It was the most beautiful thing Beol had ever heard, though there were no words.

They hit a particularly high note, and Dr. Bloop joined in. The puppy began to howl loudly, trying to follow along.

Beck looked horrified. "Bloop, be quiet." He picked the puppy up and tried to hold his mouth closed.

Bloop was determined and shook him off. Soon enough, the other dogs attending the wedding with their owners added their own howls.

Beol saw Wyatt turn red and hide his face when his dog, Luna, started howling happily from her seat with Wyatt's mate, Morgan.

Sebastian covered his mouth and shook with suppressed giggles. Their own dog was howling with the others, and as soon as he made eye contact with Alois, the couple practically rolled with laughter.

The Sirens' song changed, adding a drop of humor and silliness, and both of Selene's siblings grinned as they continued to sing happily.

Beol barely heard Tinker's giggle, but she was

rolling around, so he knew she was just as amused as he was.

The song came to an end and the dogs quieted.

The Fallon minister finished the ceremony, and the wedding party marched back down the aisle.

Hack patted Beck's puppy on the head. "Dr. Bloop, you added a little something special to that song, and you're now my favorite grandpuppy."

Beck winced. "Don't encourage him. That was so embarrassing, Bloop."

Tinker poked her head over the brim of Beol's hat and tittered softly. She flew down and sat on Bloop's head. The puppy sat perfectly still and rolled his eyes up, trying to see her.

Hack's mouth dropped open again. "What the hell is that?"

"She's so pretty!" Rizzie darted over and crouched beside Bloop.

Xu joined her. "She's a fairy, Mom. Like in the book Grandma reads Rizzie and me."

"Is that Icarus?" Selene moved to block Bloop and the fairy from sight of the moving crowd.

"No, this is Tinker." Beol shook his head. Did Tinker look like a son designed to be a warrior? Selene lacked basic observational skills and obviously wouldn't be a good mother to Icarus.

Hack slapped Beck's arm. "How many did you make?"

"Only our three children and then Tinker and another fairy. The fairies aren't quite like the others.

They're sentient, but more animal than person. Kinda like Princess."

"Why does Beol have her?" Selene kicked Beol's leg, and it almost buckled. "Why not me?"

Beck looked at him and blushed. "After I made her, I told her all about finding my mate. She wanted to be Beol's buddy." Beck gripped his tail. "I got four more like her ready to polish up and finish, but I'm afraid. What if someone steals them and tries to sell them? They need to be able to *choose* their friends, like Tinker did."

Beol scowled. He hated that his mate was afraid for his precious creations. "I won't let them be taken."

Selene's eyes grew predatory. "What would you do, assassin, if someone took Beck's creations?"

Beol met her gaze, unafraid, and let his ruthlessness show. "I'd kill them."

Her face remained expressionless, but she tilted her head again. "I like you."

Hack frowned. "No. He's not gentle and sweet. You can't like him, Selene. Beck needs gentle and sweet."

Beck rolled his eyes. "Beol is gentle and sweet."

Bendix popped up behind them. "Boss man is so gentle and sweet you wouldn't believe it."

"Guild Master Beol?" Noe pushed through the chairs. "Are you talking about *our* boss man? Don't you remember that hit on Port Broacia?"

"Ignore them, Beck." Beol picked up Bloop and Tinker and pulled his mate away from their friends. "Let's go get some food."

"Can we dance?" Beck's eyes lit up, and Beol groaned.

"I've never really danced before, but Hay showed me a few of the basics a couple of days ago."

"He can't even dance." Hack shook his head. "Shameful."

"Daddy, you can't dance good either." Rizzie poked her father in the leg. "You're supposed to be nice to Mr. Beol today. Daddy Leti said so."

Hack gave his daughter a disgruntled look. "Fine. Dance with me first, Beol. I'll show you some moves too. Despite what *some* say, I'm an excellent dancer."

A half an hour later, Beol discovered that Hack was *not* an excellent dancer. Beol's feet ached from being stepped on. At least he now knew how not to dance. He really did enjoy just swaying back and forth on the dance floor with Beck.

He settled his head against Beck's chest and listened to the steady beat of his heart. "This is nice."

Beck sighed happily. "It really is."

After a while, Beol left his mate with Pris and Hay. He was showing off his new welding torch.

Beol picked up Dr. Bloop and headed for the restroom. The first one he came to had a long line, so he walked around the gardens, searching for another.

Sobbing caught his attention.

Beol silently moved behind a large bush covered in purple and white flowers. "Sebastian? What's wrong?"

Beol crouched next to the shaman. Sebastian sat on a towel, with his knees pulled to his chin. Mustachio was beside him, trilling soothingly.

Tinker flitted over and sat on Sebastian's knee, chattering worriedly.

"Nothing." Sebastian quickly wiped his eyes and gave Beol a strained smile.

Beol arched a brow and waited silently.

Sebastian huffed. "It's just that today has been so beautiful and perfect. I love Alois more than anything in the galaxy."

"Those sobs weren't happy."

Sebastian's eyes filled again. "I can't help thinking about Union Station. The Queen killed all those people, decimated a planet, because I made her angry. All those people are dead because of me, and here I am, having the happiest moment of my life."

"Don't make yourself a martyr." Beol gave Sebastian a hard look. "You know better than that, Sebastian."

"She went there because of me, Beol. Me."

"Union Station was a central trading hub that had a poor relationship with Vextonar."

"So? She stood outside my parents' house. She killed them."

"Did you know that Vextonar is handling all of the clean-up? In two weeks, they've already created a spaceport completely under their control."

"What?"

"Who pulls the Queen's strings, Sebastian?"

Sebastian's eyes widened, and he gasped. "Humans First. Vextonar's population is mostly human."

"I'm not arguing that she didn't go there and destroy Union Station out of anger at the death of her

Element. What I'm telling you is that Union Station's destruction was likely planned long ago."

Sebastian closed his eyes and swallowed hard.

"Sebastian, even if she chose that planet because of your parents, its destruction is still on her head. The events that led her there don't matter. She's the one who chose to do it." Beol patted the shaman's knee. "Do you blame Verion Morrick for your cousin's death?"

Sebastian frowned. "What? Of course not. The owners of the lab were the ones that murdered her." Sebastian rolled his eyes. "Okay. I see what you're saying."

Beol jumped up. "Now, clean yourself up and get your ass out there. Alois is probably looking for you."

Sebastian sighed and let Beol help him up. "You're kind of amazing, Beol. You know that, right?"

"Would you mind telling Hack that?"

Sebastian gave a short bark of laughter that cut off when Cordelia and Quinn ran past their bush.

"I can't believe someone set the cake table on fire," Cordelia said, voice decidedly grumpy.

"Someone? Really? That's what you're going with? We couldn't possibly know who did it?" Quinn sounded skeptical.

Beol sighed. "I leave for five minutes and my mate sets something on fire."

7

*B*eck ran his hands up and down Beol's back. His mate straddled his lap, rocking against him as they kissed. Beol's mouth was hot, and he tasted so damn good. If Beck could, he'd shift and roll all over his mate to cover himself in Beol's scent.

Beck's hips arched, and his hands found their way to Beol's muscular ass.

Beol was small, but pure muscle, and Beck hoped the man didn't mind Beck's soft belly. He'd put on a few pounds over the last year since he'd been on the station with Ma and Icarus's cooking.

"Dad, are you guys going to kiss all night? I made a cake since you didn't get any at the wedding this morning."

Beol smiled against Beck's lips.

Beck pulled away. "Sorry, Rus. That cake smells good."

Icarus leaned against the wall, arms crossed, while

Tinker perched on his shoulder. Bloop sat at his feet and gave them an accusing look.

"Can you take a break from kissing?"

Beck sighed dramatically. "Maybe."

Beol hopped up. "Come on, Sparky. That cake really does smell good."

Beck leaned back on the couch and watched Beol walk into the kitchen. After their abrupt departure from the wedding, Beck had suggested a movie back at the house. They had cuddled on the couch, surrounded by the androids and their friends, and watched a newly released mystery.

When Becca and Gregor had headed home, Beck hadn't been able to resist another taste of Beol. He hadn't even noticed the others going downstairs and Icarus moving around the kitchen.

"Dad?" Icarus watched him in amusement.

Beck blushed. "Sorry. He's distracting."

Icarus snickered and brought him a slice of cake. He sat on the couch and leaned his head against Beck's shoulder as he ate.

"Sometimes I wish I could eat."

Beck paused mid-chew, filled with guilt.

Icarus snorted. "Don't look like that, Dad. I'm not Grell, Human, Fallon, or any other species. My source of energy is entirely different, so there was no need to build me to eat. Hmm, I wonder if there are species out there that don't eat."

Beck knew his grin was goofy as hell. Icarus always wondered about funny things. Come to think of it, so did Beck and he *was* Icarus's dad.

"I only know of one species that doesn't consume food of some sort." Beol sat on Beck's other side and leaned into him, plate of cake in hand. "There's a planet on the edge of the Radiant System called Eloide."

Beck kissed the top of his head. "I've never heard of it."

"Who lives there?" Icarus asked.

"They're called Eloidions, and they're very reclusive. Half-Moon was hired to kill the political rival of our client. Bendix and I were given the hit."

"Was the target a bad person?" Icarus sounded sad, so Beck wrapped an arm around his shoulders.

"In this case, yes, he was. My father never cared about good or bad, just the amount of money the client would pay. I'm far more selective as Guild Master."

Icarus sighed in relief. "What are the Eloidions like?"

Beol looked thoughtful. "The easiest way to describe them is as plant people."

Icarus gasped. "Photosynthesis!"

"Yeah. They're an interesting species."

"That's what you and the girls are," Beck told Icarus. "An interesting new species."

Beol nodded. "I can't wait to see what you all accomplish."

Icarus smiled, pleased, and hugged Beck, burrowing into his side.

"The Eloide job was crazy." Bendix sat and propped his feet up on the coffee table. He had his own piece of cake.

"When did you get here?" Beck asked, looking around.

He could barely hear Noe and Moyra in the kitchen. They hadn't been here when Beck and the others finished the movie.

"Ninetta and Wolfe messaged us that there was cake and sentient androids." Bendix moaned. "This is so good, Icarus."

Icarus beamed. "Thanks."

"I didn't hear you come in." Beol sounded so disgruntled, and Beck had to struggle not to laugh at him.

Bendix snorted. "You were kind of distracted. By the way, boss man, we are completely with you on the whole protect Icarus and the girls thing." Bendix took another bite and swallowed.

Beol smirked. "I never doubted that."

"I personally think the Lord Admiral will bend over backwards to protect Icarus, Sax, and Meggie. If he doesn't though, then Half-Moon will." Bendix burped. "Damn, Icarus, your cooking is the fucking best."

"Bendix, can you at least pretend you have manners?" Hay sat across from him.

Beck finished his cake, then leaned back. He really liked the Half-Moon folks, but he missed Hack and Selene and wished he had told them about Icarus earlier. He hadn't wanted them to get in trouble with the Council. He wished they were here to see this, to get to know Hay and Bendix.

He knew this was where he belonged – here with

his mate and his son. He had to believe that tomorrow's meeting with the Council wouldn't change that.

———

THE NEXT MORNING, BECK WAS ON THE COUCH AGAIN, kissing Beol. He couldn't get enough of his mate's taste.

"Do I need to get the water hose?" Hack asked sullenly from the front door.

Beck yelped, startled, and started to move, but Beol growled and held Beck's head still for one more long, wet kiss.

Beol lifted his head and glared at Hack. "What are you doing here? We don't meet the Council for two more hours."

Gregor poked his head out of the basement door. "Actually, we meet the Council in thirty minutes. You've been making out for almost three hours. Is it safe to come out yet?"

"Three hours?" Beol looked at his communicator.

"It feels more like twenty-four hours," Becca said dryly from behind Gregor. "I swear, Beol, you're either holding Beck's lips hostage or talking to Icarus. When do you sleep?"

"Thirty minutes, guys." Hack looked at Beck pointedly. "Are we even going to get to meet Icarus before the Council does? Selene is outside."

"Selene?" Beck stood, keeping Beol in his arms.

His mate slowly slid down his body, threatening to distract him again.

"Just be happy we kept your secret, or everyone would be here. Blue Solace has your back, Beck."

"Dad?" Icarus's voice came from the basement.

Beck rushed past Gregor and Becca. "Rus? Do you need me?"

Icarus stood with Meggie and Sax. "Do we look alright? We let Meggie dress us." Each of them wore formal business clothing.

Beck grinned. "You all look like accountants."

Meggie shuddered. "Don't remind me."

"We want them to take us seriously." Icarus bit his lip.

Beck rushed forward and hugged his son. "They'll love you, Icarus." He grabbed Meggie and Sax, pulling them into his hug. "They'll love all of you."

Beol came down the stairs. "If they don't realize how amazing the three of you are, they'll have Half-Moon to deal with."

"There you go," Beck said, letting them go. "We have a team of assassins on our side. Are you kids ready?"

"We aren't kids." Meggie frowned but leaned up and kissed his cheek. "We're as ready as we're going to get."

Beol walked Meggie and Sax up the stairs, and Beck turned back to Icarus. "I'm sorry that I've been so distracted lately. I should have been down here helping you get ready."

"You just met your mate, Dad. Don't sweat it." Icarus's smile was gentle and sweet, just like his boy. "I know you love me."

"I do love you." Beck hugged him one more time, then followed him upstairs and outside.

Hack's mouth hung open as he stared at Meggie and Sax.

"Don't be rude, Hack," Beol said.

Meanwhile, Meggie and Sax were looking around, wide-eyed, and Beck felt like shit. He should have figured out a way for them to leave the damn house.

Gregor and Becca herded the women toward a shuttle while Beol waited on them, Bloop in his arms.

"We brought a private shuttle." Selene held her hand out to Icarus. "Come along, son."

"Son?" Icarus tilted his head, looking eerily like Selene.

"Beck explained he modeled you after me." Selene looked him over. "I see the similarities. He should have told me sooner, but I've decided to forgive him."

Icarus grinned. "Okay, Mom."

Beol cleared his throat and shot Selene a poisonous look. "Are we ready?"

"We are." Icarus puffed his chest out. He smirked at Sax and Meggie. "Hear that? I have two dads and a mom already."

Beck led him to the shuttle. "Dads?"

Icarus smiled shyly. "Well, Beol will be my dad, right?"

Beol shot Selene a smug look. "Yes, Icarus. I will be."

Sax looked at Gregor. "Dad, when do I get a mom?"

Gregor winced. "It may be a while, sweetie. My dating record isn't great."

"I'll let you borrow my mom, Sax." Icarus sent Sax an adoring look. "I just got her, but I know she's great."

Beck sat up straight. *Oh no.* Icarus was too young to be adoring anyone, *damn it.*

Meggie snickered. "That's not really how moms work, Icarus. By the way, I'm borrowing Beol. Mom dates as much as Gregor does, which is *not at all.* You have two dads, so you can spare one when I need him."

"What do you need him for?" Icarus gave her a dark look. "I just got him, so you better not break him."

A short and disturbing ride later, they arrived at the central sector where the Council was gathered in a formal conference room. Selene and Hack stayed with the androids in the private waiting area outside the door while Beck and the others went in.

A thoroughly disgruntled Fasi met them at the door. "You're here. Good. Now what the hell is going on?"

The Council gathered around the conference table, chattering as they waited. They quieted as Beck, Gregor, and Becca approached the front of the room.

"Thanks for seeing us." Beck's tail was in his hand before he realized it. He absolutely hated being the center of attention, but Icarus and the girls were worth it.

Fasi plopped in a chair. "We'll always have time for you, Beck. So, what's happening here? I didn't know you were acquainted with Becca and Gregor."

"We met in a bar." Gregor winced. "We really need to quit saying that and maybe start the story somewhere else."

Becca cleared her throat. "To clarify our purpose here, Councilmen and women, we three are friends that have created something wonderful. We need your help to protect our creations."

Councilman Delino gave her a half-smile. "The Council isn't usually called in to file a patent—not that we're not curious about what three of Charybdis Station's most brilliant citizens created."

Becca blushed, and Beck and Gregor exchanged a surprised look. Becca was the steadiest of them. She didn't *blush*.

Beck grunted. *Huh.*

Beol stepped forward, confident and calm. "What they created is completely unknown to the galaxy. It is completely unique, and they are requesting the Council's help in protecting it."

"Guild Master Beol." Delino nodded to him. He looked around at the other Council members. "You have our interest."

"We've created sentient androids," Beck blurted out. "They're our babies. You gotta help us keep them safe. Please?"

Fasi jumped up when Beck started to cry. "Beck, it'll be alright. Don't cry, son." He hugged Beck tightly.

"I'm sorry. I'm no good at talking, and this is important. They're not just some weapon that's gonna make fighting easier." Beck's face was hot with embarrassment, but his tears wouldn't stop.

Beol slipped under his arm and wrapped his arms around Beck's waist.

"I'm right with you, man." Gregor wiped his own eyes. "These are our babies. Becca, can you explain it?"

She cleared her throat. "As Beck said, we've created

sentient androids. They are not controllable or predictable. They are complete individuals who just happened to be created rather than birthed."

Councilwoman Brinanda looked at them in amazement. "Sentient?"

"Yes," Becca answered, then walked to the door. "I'll let you meet them now."

She opened the door and Hack and Selene led Icarus, Sax, and Meggie into the room.

Fasi squeezed Beck and Beol. "I won't let anyone hurt them, Beck. I promise you," he whispered. He let them go and stepped back. "Hack. You knew about this?"

"Just found out." Hack crossed his arms and glared at the Council. "Who made Beck cry?"

"No one did. Geez, Hack." Beck kept Beol in his arms but held his head high.

"Will you introduce us?" Councilman Mitchell stood, and the others followed suit.

Gregor took Sax's hand. "This is my daughter, Sax. I'm the one who planned her features and traits, but once someone is sentient, they're an individual."

Sax smiled at her dad. "Dad loves music. He wanted to create a perfect musician, so he gave me a kick-ass voice and an ability with instruments."

"She's so damn talented." Gregor grinned proudly.

"I am," she agreed, smirking. "I'm not going to be a musician though. I want to protect people. Charybdis Station isn't a mercenary station anymore." She looked over her shoulder at Beol, before again addressing the Council. "Everything has a season, and Charybdis

Station has become something more than it was. I've been training, and I'm going to be a soldier."

"Are you?" Brinanda arched a brow.

"She'll be part of my personal crew, as soon as the Lord Admiral gives his approval," Hack said.

"I'll enjoy furthering her training," Selene said, face expressionless as usual.

Mitchell grinned. "We'll see."

Becca stepped forward. "This is Meggie. I'm the one who planned her creation."

Meggie grinned at the Council and waved.

Becca laughed softly. "I wanted to create a more efficient field medic. Meggie was designed to provide injured persons with quality care, fast and effectively. I had thought she would be practical and subservient."

Meggie made a face, and the Council members chuckled.

Becca gestured to her plain clothes and short, practical hair. "If you will notice, I'm not the most stylish person. It's not something I've ever found important, so I never thought my daughter would be so consumed with fashion. I certainly didn't create her that way. She *is* her own person and deserves to be seen as an individual."

Meggie nodded firmly. "I'll happily be the most fashionable medic on Charybdis Station, but not forever. Medics have an important job, and the gods know they're needed, but I want to be a doctor. I feel I could help the most people by following in Mom's footsteps."

Hack gave an exaggerated gasp. "What? The Blue

Fleet happens to need more medics. You could join us until you go to school. Then, you can join us as a doctor."

Fasi grinned. "What a wonderful coincidence."

Beck pulled Icarus to him, wrapping an arm around his son's shoulders. Icarus looked as nervous as Beck. He had a feeling Icarus had inherited more than his creative mind.

"This is my son, Icarus. I love him more than anything."

"Oh, Beck." Fasi gave him a soft look.

"I thought he'd be like Selene, a soldier, so I made him big and gave him certain skills."

"I'm his mother," Selene said, coming to stand on Icarus's other side.

Icarus smiled shyly at the Council. "I'm not going to be a soldier though. I could fight, if I had to, but I love making food and caring for things. I love Dr. Bloop and Tinker, and I'm really good at keeping plants alive. I have a fern named Fawn."

Hack shook his head. "Imagine that. Blue Sector could always use someone to help in the gardens and at Juniper's Diner. My family alone could keep him busy as a pet-sitter and landscaper. So many possibilities."

"We've compiled the evidence of sentience we gathered after their creations," Becca said. "We know you'll need to run more tests under the surveillance of different scientists, but we would be happy to share our own findings as well."

Delino gave her a heated look. "Thank you, Dr. Rayne."

This time Fasi and Hack exchanged looks with Beck. Delino wasn't known for his *heated* looks. Beck shrugged. Who knew what would happen?

"Three complete individuals," Mitchell said. "It's a pleasure to meet each of you."

"I think we can all understand the fears you have," Delino said. "What you've done is beyond belief. Scientists have tried for millennia to create sentient beings."

Mitchell nodded. "He's quite right. Now, this raises some complicated questions, and it won't be an easy process, but if we eventually agreed to grant them citizenship, is it as a species or as three individual cases?"

"What he means is: do you intend to make more?" Brinanda watched them carefully.

Becca turned to him. "What do you say, Beck? You do the brunt of the work."

"I have made two more and started a few others that are different from the kids," he admitted.

Tinker chose that moment to poke her head out of Beol's jacket. Bloop woofed and trotted over to say hello.

Beck quickly explained Tinker and his other, smaller, creations.

"Two separate types of sentient androids," Brinanda mused. "You don't make things easy, do you?"

Beck took a deep breath. "I would love to create more like Icarus and the girls. They make the galaxy brighter, and I can't see why that would be a bad thing, but I won't as long as there's a chance they won't be seen as people."

"Then the best way forward will be to aim for citizenship as a species," Delino said. "What is their species?"

"Bracken," Gregor and Becca said at the same time. They shared a grin.

"Gregor and I talked about it last night," Becca said. "Beck Brackenstone gave us our girls, well, young women, as Meggie would say."

"I like it." Fasi whooped and looked at the Council. "Want to make history?"

Brinanda rolled her eyes and laughed with the rest of the Council. "We knew you'd bring the station in a new direction, Fasi, but this isn't something I ever foresaw."

"What about Tinker?" Beol smiled when his fairy flew to him and perched on his head.

Councilwoman Jalina gave Tinker a thoughtful look. "Beck's smaller creations aren't like the others, but they aren't simple androids. What about starting the process to make them a protected animal species? We've done that with the Radollia on Grellweir."

"That would fit them best, I think." Beck nibbled his lip. "Tinker has emotions and is super smart, but she's not reasoning like a person. She reminds me of Dr. Bloop."

"They will need a separate name," Jalina said. "We must differentiate them from the Bracken."

"How about Charybdis Fyrlings?" Becca looked between Beck and Gregor. "We can't call them all fairies. There's that toad-looking thing you've been working on."

"How many are you planning to make, Beck?" Hack grinned at him.

"I haven't finished any more," Beck said, blushing. He had four ready to go and several in different stages of completion. They were all so adorable.

"I would like to make one thing clear," Beol said. "You will find that they are sentient, but until you are able to grant them citizenship and recognition as a species, the Bracken and the Fyrlings are under the protection of Half-Moon."

"That isn't a bad idea," Fasi said. "I would love to believe that every person on our station would respect Beck and his creations, but I've been disappointed before."

"Shall we vote on beginning the process?" Delino looked over the Council. "While the Lord Admiral does have the final say, it will hold weight if we show our own support."

"I second the call for a vote," Mitchell said with a grin. "As Fasi said, let's make history."

"Who agrees to begin the process of proving the sentience of the Bracken and the Charybdis Fyrlings?" Fasi looked around the room.

All six Council members raised their hands.

8

eol held Beck's hand as they walked back to the shuttle. The whole group was silent. The Council had given their support, but there was a lot left to do. One thing in particular worried Beol.

"Beck, can we talk alone for a minute?"

Beck nodded, and they fell behind the others. "What's wrong? This went really well, didn't it?"

"It went a lot better than expected. Every Council member seemed to be supportive." Beol took both of Beck's hands in his own. "You and I are mates, and very soon, we'll be lovers."

Beck blushed but grinned. "I like the sound of that."

"We also need to be able to protect the Bracken and Fyrlings."

"Yeah, we do." Beck's face was full of misery. "I want them to be able to leave the house."

"I want you all to move into the Half-Moon neighborhood." Beck's face lit up. Beol continued, "Hack and your friends can't keep an eye on Rus and the others like we can. No one enters the neighborhood who hasn't been approved by me personally, and someone is always on patrol."

Beck's shoulders slumped. "You want me to move in just so you can protect Icarus, Meggie, and Sax?"

Beol stroked his cheek. "No. I want *you* to move in because I hate it when we're apart. I want Icarus to move in because he's going to be my son soon. I want the others to move in so we can keep them safe."

"I'll need a workshop."

"Pops has already marked a large room in the back of the house for your workshop. He pointed it out last time he visited."

"I can't believe they visited you and they didn't tell me." Beck made a face.

"I can't believe you didn't tell me about my grandbaby!"

Beol and Beck turned around to find Ma and Pops standing behind them. They both looked furious.

"We just got a message from Fasi telling us you have a son named Icarus," Pops said. "What's going on, young man?"

"Fasi's a bigmouth," Beck said, pouting.

Beol chuckled. "You sound like Meggie."

"Beol! You're in trouble too, mister." Ma's hands went to her hips, and Beol was reminded of Leti. Fuck, he would probably be doing that too soon enough.

"I'm sorry," he mumbled and bent to pick up Bloop.

"It's complicated, Ma." Beck grabbed her hand and started tugging. "Come on. Let's get to the house, and I'll explain."

———

"I'M SO PROUD OF YOU, BECK." POPS SNIFFLED. "I CAN'T believe the three of you did this. I'm just, gods, I'm just so amazed."

"I knew that mind of yours was special," Ma said, tears streaming down her face as she hugged Icarus to her. "I just didn't realize it was this special. Oh, Icarus, I'm so happy to meet you."

"Grandma, come on. I want to show you my recipe box. Dad said you keep a digital copy and a physical copy of yours, so I did the same with mine. Dad built me a really nice box and everything."

Ma sobbed and hugged him harder.

"You'd think she didn't have any grandchildren already." Beck watched his parents worriedly.

Beol squeezed his hand. "I think she would be this happy over any new grandchild."

"I'm sorry I didn't tell you all earlier," Beck said. "I knew politics and shit would come up, and I didn't want to get you all involved."

"Son, we're your family. We're already involved." Pops hugged Beck. "We forgive you though. Just don't go creating more grandchildren for us without telling us."

"Becca, Gregor, and I work well together. We've made other things too. There's this one project we've been working on that involves bots. I seriously love it, Pops. You'll get a kick out of it."

Becca and Gregor left their corner in the basement.

"Beol," Gregor said, eyes pleading. "I know you two

said Beck and the kids are moving in with you, but would it be possible for Becca and me to rent a couple of houses or apartments in your neighborhood? We could be with our kids that way."

Meggie stood behind them, hands pressed together, begging. "Please, Beol?"

Beol nodded. "I have to run it by the guild first, but I don't see any problems with it."

"We'll need to move your workshop." Pops patted Beck on the back. "Show me these bots, son. Your ma just stole Icarus."

Beol turned around. Ma and Icarus were disappearing into the kitchen.

"I'll leave you two to the workshop. I'm going to go talk to the guild now. The sooner we can move them all to Half-Moon, the better."

"I'm still not convinced that's the best idea," Hack said, scowling. "My crew is perfectly capable of protecting Icarus and the girls."

Selene shook her head. "I want to agree with you, but our neighborhood is a family neighborhood. It isn't patrolled by well-trained assassins."

"Fire and Princess patrol the area," Hack protested.

"They can also visit Beol's neighborhood." Selene poked Hack in the cheek. "No more scowling. Beck loves Beol already. I can tell. My son and his friends will be better guarded with Beol, and Beol needs to be near his people. We would be upset if you and Leti moved away from us. His guild wants him nearby."

Hack scowled and crossed his arms. "Fine, but you better let us all come visit."

"Anytime, Hack," Beck said. "You guys are my family."

"Yes. Family." Beol winced.

"Just realized what you've gotten into, huh?" Pops smacked his shoulder. "Too late now, Beol."

A few minutes later, Beol and Tinker headed for the tram. The Fyrling sat on his shoulder, chittering in his ear.

"Hey, boss man." Bendix popped into view beside him after deactivating his shield. "That went well."

Tinker squawked and jumped onto Beol's head.

Wolfe, Noe, and Moyra appeared beside them.

"The Council surprised me," Wolfe signed.

"I thought for sure they would try to take Icarus and the girls into custody," Noe said, frowning. "It went a little too easily, if you ask me."

"Charybdis Station is different," Moyra said thoughtfully. "The Lord Admiral adores Beck, and the Council members are fairly reasonable."

"We'll keep an eye on them," Beol said. "Beck told me they encrypted the files they plan to send to the Council, and Gregor added extra safety precautions."

"The guy knows his stuff," Moyra said. "What I've found on him is impressive. He's also completely loyal to Charybdis Station. A Charybdis couple raised him after his parents were killed in the Sugarworm System."

"What about Becca?" Beol didn't want to think either Becca or Gregor would betray Beck, but he had learned a long time ago people weren't always what they seemed.

"Fucking brilliant," Moyra said. "That woman is impressive as hell. Her family lives on Fallow and are very supportive. She's not from here, but there is absolutely no indication that she would want to betray either the station or Beck."

"Are you all alright with them moving to the neighborhood?" Beol would ask everyone, but these four, along with Hay, Ninetta, and Otto, were his closest friends.

"They'll make good additions," Wolfe signed. "I'd like to have Gregor look at our security."

"Let's get everyone together and make the announcement." Beol left the tram, and they started toward his house. "I want Beck and Icarus with me tonight. If someone is going to try something, they'll try it soon."

———

"I can't believe we're moved in." Beck looked around the house in amazement.

"There's like a thousand of us," Dannol said, carrying another box into the kitchen. "That comes in handy when you've got to move stuff."

Princess Buttercup walked past them with Sami and Pepper, two of Leti's kids, riding on his back. Tinker sat on the large Fire Veil Dragon's head, trilling a battle march.

"Then again, sometimes having us all around is a bit much," Dannol added, snickering at the look on Beol's face.

"Their bedroom is the third door on the left, Will." Leti stood in the hallway, directing everyone. The slow-moving fairy curled up on his shoulder. She'd chosen her person the second she saw Leti.

"How do you know the layout of the whole house?" Hack grumbled as he picked up the three boxes he had just set down.

"Beol and I are best friends now," Let said smugly.

Beol scowled when Beck laughed. "You mean you come over daily and invade my privacy."

Leti shrugged. "That's what best friends do. Ask Draif."

"At least he doesn't send you messages about Hack's dick," Draif said from the kitchen. "Sometimes it's poems, and other times it's colorful descriptions."

Beol shuddered, and Beck laughed harder.

Five Grell women pushed through the front door. Three were yellow and two were green, but they all looked a whole lot like Ma.

"Where's Beol?" The oldest one scanned the room until her eyes landed on Beol. "There's our grumpy little kitty."

"Nala, don't call him that." Beck stomped his foot. "What are you all doing here?"

Nala scowled. "We've waited long enough. You're our baby brother, and we have a right to interrogate your mate."

"Ma said we have a new nephew too," one of the green women said. "Beck, why would you keep our nephew from us?"

Beck gave him a stricken look. "I'm so sorry, Beol. I'm so sorry they're here."

"Now, now," Nala said with a smile on her face. "Don't scare the kitty. We'll be gentle."

The five women surrounded him, and before Beol knew what was happening, he found himself alone with them in the downstairs bathroom.

Nala pushed him, and he sat on the toilet, looking up at all of them. "I'm Nala, the oldest. This is Jyra, Bwenna, Dian, and Sola."

"We just have a few questions," Sola said. "We've already completed a comprehensive background check, but there are a few things we want to hear straight from you."

"You can't kill any of us either, so we'll ask everything we want." Nala smirked.

"Nala," Sola said. "The man does deserve *some* privacy. Well, as long as he doesn't hurt Beck. If that was to happen, we'd discover all of his weaknesses and make his life a living hell before finally murdering him and throwing his body in Charybdis Station's fiery core."

"Oh, the things we could do to you," Jyra said.

They all sighed happily.

"This doesn't feel *gentle* to me." Beol frowned. He really shouldn't like these women.

Dian cleared her throat. "Question one – Can you take care of yourself? Beck doesn't need some man to take care of. He's got more important things to do than pander to your every wish."

"I've been caring for myself for a very long time now. There will be no pandering."

Nala gave him a hard look. "Question two – We know the guild is wealthy, so we aren't worried about that. We want to know if you like children. Beck loves kids and needs to have a million of his own."

"My guild *is* very wealthy and each of us draws a high salary. I can provide for not only myself, but also for Beck and all of our children."

"I didn't ask if you could provide for them."

Beol snarled. "I don't know if I like children. I've only ever been around Pris and Otto's son."

"Do you like him?"

"Of course! He's part of my guild."

Nala grinned. "Well, there you go. A million babies better be on the way soon."

Sola pushed her sister out of the way. "Enough of that. Question three – Are you patient? Beck's shy and gets rattled easily. You need to be patient, so you don't make things worse for him. He's highly creative and needs to be given the chance to express himself."

"I can be patient, yes. Beck is brilliant, and I fully appreciate that fact."

"Question four," Jyra said. "We know you kill people for a living, but that's business. Would you ever resort to violence during a fight with Beck? I suggest you think really hard before answering."

"I would *never* hurt Beck." Beol shook his head. "I would never physically hurt him, and I would never purposely cause him emotional pain. Never."

Bwenna stepped forward. The green Grell was the

youngest of the sisters. "Okay, this is the most important one. Question five – Do you love Beck?"

Beol blinked and his mouth hung open. He couldn't possibly love Beck yet, could he? He had kept his heart hidden for so long. A few weeks couldn't possibly be long enough to unbury it.

Nala patted his cheek. "I think we just broke him."

"We were being so gentle though," Jyra exclaimed.

———

THAT NIGHT, BEOL SAT ON HIS BED AND WAITED FOR Beck to finish brushing his teeth. He knew Beck was worried about him. Beol had been quiet ever since Bwenna asked her question.

"All done!" Beck bounced into the room, wearing only his pajama pants. "Are you sure you don't mind me sleeping in here with you?"

Beol shook his head. "You belong here."

He held his hand out to Beck and drew the large man to him. Beck settled beside him on the bed, and Beol leaned up, kissing him softly. Beck's taste had haunted Beol ever since their first kiss.

"Beol? If we keep kissing, things are gonna happen."

"I like things." Beol kissed him again. "I can bottom or top. I enjoy either, and as long as I'm with you, I'm happy. I think I'm addicted to your fur."

Beck groaned. "I know what I want to do, but can you show me?"

"What do you want?"

"I want inside you. Then, I want you inside me. I want everything."

Beol smiled softly and straddled him. "We'll start with you in me. We have every night for the rest of our lives, Beck. We've got time."

"You're really mine, huh?"

Beol didn't answer him. He couldn't voice it, not yet.

Instead, he kissed his way down Beck's solid chest, stopping to appreciate his dark green nipples, then his soft belly.

"You don't mind that I'm fat?"

Beol snorted and looked up. "Seriously? A soft belly doesn't make you fat, Beck. Even if you were, you're still my Beck. I think my dick could point the way to you even if the whole station went dark."

Beck smiled, and Beol's stomach fluttered. Damn, that smile always did him in.

He scooted down Beck's body, hands smoothing over fine green fur. He pulled Beck's pants down and hummed. He was a lucky man.

"Can I see you?" Beck's blush traveled all the way down his chest.

Beol stood and pulled off his clothes. He wasn't shy or worried. He knew Beck would want him despite the scars and burns on his body.

"How can you be so beautiful?" Beck's hands skimmed up Beol's sides, his dark green eyes reverent.

"Most people think Wolfe's the beautiful one." Beol knew his chin was too pointy, and his face a little too rough to be called beautiful.

Beck shook his head. "They must not have seen you."

Beol's dick hardened painfully, and he reached over to grab the lube out of the side table. "Compliment me later, Sparky. I really need you in me."

"Won't hear me complaining." Beck stroked his dick, and Beol straddled his lap.

Beck's hands slid over Beol's ass, and a slick finger found his hole. He pushed back against it, and Beck dropped his head onto Beol's shoulder.

"I'm not gonna last long. Nope. I'm not. This is gonna be embarrassing."

Beol reached back and held Beck's hand, guiding his mate's fingers into his body. "Don't worry, Sparky. I'm not going to last long either."

When he was stretched enough, he lowered himself onto Beck's dick, slowly filling up. He groaned as his ass hit Beck's thighs.

Beck gasped against Beol's neck, hands on Beol's hips. He drew him up, then Beol slammed himself down. They both cried out.

"Again, again, again." Beck moaned and kissed him.

Beol set the pace, quickly riding Beck until he came, splattering all over Beck's stomach.

Beck growled, then lifted him up and rolled Beol to his back. He bent Beol's legs, giving himself more access and pounded into Beol.

Beol felt him come and hot seed filled him up.

Beck collapsed against him, panting hard. "When can we do that again?"

9

Beck whistled a happy tune as he fiddled with a project in his new workshop. It had taken a few days, but Pops, Lerais, and Hazel had helped him finish setting up. He was putting the finishing touches on one of his Fyrlings now. Each of them was unique and precious. Gods, he loved them all.

He had finished another Fyrling that was similar in looks to Tinker. She had chosen Pris as her person, and Beck couldn't have been happier with that choice.

His remaining three Fyrlings were different though, but he knew they'd find someone to love.

Icarus poked his head into the workshop. "Dad, Ninetta and I are going to help Ma and Pris with the neighborhood garden. Okay?"

Beck lifted his goggles. "Have fun, sweetheart. Do you want to take Bloop with you?"

Beck's puppy sat on his bed, looking bored. He perked up when he heard his name.

"Oh yeah." Icarus came in and scooped up Bloop. "We need to get you a straw hat Bloop, so you can be a farmer when you're working in the gardens with me."

They wandered out the door, and Beck turned back to the Fyrling. This one wasn't a fairy. He was a little bigger than Tinker, but not by much. He had the body of a horse, but the head and wings of an Old-Earth eagle.

Beck had gotten the idea from Leti's book of myths. He had seen a picture of a hippogriff and had wanted to make one right then. He wondered what this Fyrling would be like.

He and Gregor had given up on trying to program personalities into their kids. They could program them with certain knowledge, but their personalities were too ingrained in their sentience.

"Beck?" Hack's voice came from the front of the house.

"In my workshop."

A few minutes later, Hack came in. "Hey."

Beck smiled at his friend. "Did you know sex is amazing?"

Hack winced. "Yes. I did know that. Do I need to know that you and Beol have sex? No. No, I do not."

"A healthy sex life is good for a relationship, Hack." Beck grinned at his friend's discomfort. "There's no reason not to talk about it. Beol and I had sex four times last night. Four!"

"Please, no more." Hack slumped into one of the many chairs scattered around the room.

Beck chuckled. "Alright, alright. What did you need?"

"I just left a meeting with Dad and the other generals. We know something needs to be done about HF and the Queen."

Beck nodded. HF, or Humans First, was a coalition of wealthy humans. They hated non-human species and had participated in the murder of billions so far through the alliance with the Crellic Queen.

"Honestly, we're at a standstill right now." Hack sighed and leaned back. "We can't physically approach her or even get near her without her knowing. Death isn't sure that he and Fire can take out both her and Earth."

"Kill her from a distance?"

"We haven't been successful in converting the poison Wyatt developed into something that can be shot from a distance."

"Can he make a different poison?"

"That's what they're working on, but it apparently isn't as easy as Wyatt made it look when he created the first one."

"What other ways can we kill her?"

"Her body will heal as quickly as her Elements did. Decapitation would work, but again, we'd have to get close."

"She would see an android too. Sebastian says he can see their threads when he's in the spirit world. Hmm. Grenades might slow her down."

"If they land the right way and we get lucky." Hack

rubbed his hands over his face. "We'll figure it out. We just don't have a lot of time. Each day that goes by is another day she could be destroying a world. *Fuck*, we don't even know the full connection between her and HF."

"She's on Genarg though, right?"

"That's what Beol's scouts say. The planet is swarming with mercenaries too, probably hired by HF."

"Anyone we know?"

"No one good."

"We'll figure it out, Hack. We have to." Beck frowned.

"We will. Now cheer me up, Beckie Boo. What's that thing you were talking to Pops about the other day. With the bots?"

"Oh. It's really something." Beck opened a drawer and pulled out a long, thin, piece of flexible metal. "So, it's linked to me since I've been working on it. We don't have an official name for it yet."

He pressed it against the side of his face, starting at the tip of his hair line. It ran all the way down to his chin. He felt it attach to his face.

"It's really kind of simple. You know how Lucas's robotic arm and leg are linked to him?"

"Yeah. He moves them just like he would his real arm and leg."

"So, this gadget links to me, but lets me access pre-programed bots instead of robotic prostheses."

"Huh?"

Beck sighed. "Watch."

Beck focused and three of the small, circular bots on the shelf above his worktable rose into the air.

"You're doing that?"

They zipped down and started circling Beck. "Yeah. It's pretty great. I have six bots and my boots linked to this headpiece, but I could link even more. It takes some time to learn how to use them though. Gregor and I like to play with them. Becca says we're big kids."

"Gregor isn't your best friend now, is he?"

"Aww, Hack, are you jealous?" Beck grinned, and one of the bots flew to Hack and released a stream of bubbles over him. "He's coming over in a few minutes too. Are you gonna get grumpy?"

"Of course, I'm jealous. You belong to me and Selene. Now, we have to share you with Beol and Icarus too." He arched a brow. "Your bot blows bubbles? That's really useful, Beck."

"You know I didn't get an attitude when you found Leti and had all your kids."

"You make it sound like we hatched them out or something."

"You know what I mean. It's like you're replacing Selene and me with new, smarter best friends."

Beck fell against his worktable, laughing. "Oh gods. Becca and Gregor are my smart friends, and you and Selene are my brawler friends."

"Laughing at me? Really?" More bubbles blew over Hack's head.

"You and Selene will always be my best friends, you idiot."

"You're right. I'm being stupid. I'm just attached to you and Selene." He sighed. "Icarus is great, and Beol isn't really *that* bad. I don't know about the others. We'll see."

"I knew you loved me," Beol said from the doorway.

Beck sent his bot to blow bubbles over Beol too.

"This is what you do in your workshop all day?"

Beck grinned. "I really need to show you what my boots can do."

Hack and Beol looked at Beck's plain, black boots. His black pants were tucked into them, so they were on full display.

Beol's comm beeped, and he looked at it. "Fuck. There's been a breach in our security. Where's Icarus?"

They grabbed their weapons and ran for the door.

"He's in the garden with Ninetta, Ma, and Pris. Sax is training with Selene and Bendix in the training center, and Meggie is studying at home with Becca. Tinker?"

"Napping in that huge fairy house you built her." They passed it as they ran through the living room. It took up the space in front of the windows.

When they got to the yard, they could see the neighborhood's community garden six houses down. A few of Beol's assassins were fighting a large group of shielded strangers.

With their special shields, Beck knew they had more Half-Moon assassins fighting than they saw.

One attacker's head was seemingly sliced off all on its own. *Yep. Invisibility shields are awesome,* Beck thought as they headed toward the fight.

Beck could barely see Icarus and Ma's heads over the fighting. He noticed a familiar yellow Grell too. Nala was in shifted form beside Ma.

His eyes met Icarus's furious face. "Dad! There's too many of them."

Beol passed them shields. "Remember to activate them."

Nala dove in front of Ma and yelped when an attacker stabbed her. She fell to the ground, and Beck howled.

"I want them to fucking see me coming." Beck focused and called his bots to him, then activated his shield. The six bots circled him, waiting for orders.

He knelt and pushed a button on his boots, then shot into the air, jumping high, aimed toward the fight.

"What the fuck, Beck?" Beol scowled at him as he soared away.

Hack whooped loudly, then kept running down the street toward the fight with Beol.

Beck landed in the middle of the fighting and started firing his phasers. His bots zipped through the tangle of bodies, firing shots, shooting electric bolts, and expelling bursts of flame.

Blades grew out of his bubble bot, and Beck sent it twirling through the group of men near Nala. It sliced into them, targeting vulnerable areas while it flooded the area with bubbles.

"Beck!" His ma's voice was full of anger. "Nala's hurt, Gregor and Bloop got shot, and Darya's here with Pris."

Beck saw her through the fighting. His ma stood tall, guarding Gregor and the others. She fired a phaser she must have picked up from somewhere with surprising accuracy.

He tried to push toward them, but there were a lot of attackers, far more than he had initially thought.

Beol was an invisible force of nature and cleared the path toward their family. Beck couldn't see him, but he could see the aftermath of his mate.

He focused on his boots and jumped again, landing on top of a black clad figure fighting with Icarus.

His son fired shots from his wrists, taking down another attacker, then grabbed yet another and quickly twisted his head around, breaking his neck.

"Dad, Ninetta gave us shields when the attack started, but she and Gregor got overwhelmed. Gregor shielded her. He's hurt bad. Bloop lay on top of Darya right from the start and got shot."

Beck grunted, then focused on the fight and pushed his worry away. They needed to finish this fast.

As more of Half-Moon arrived, the tides turned. Sax jumped into the fray alongside Selene and Bendix, and Beck knew the fight wouldn't last much longer.

His bots flew over the group and picked off attackers while he fought more and headed toward Ma and the others.

Ninetta stood over Nala and Gregor with the help of her crutch, a phaser in each hand.

With more of Half-Moon joining every second, the fighting ended quickly, and Beck knew it had taken maybe five minutes for them to take out what looked to be around sixty attackers.

Half-Moon knew their way around a phaser and a blade.

Nala shifted and sat up, hand pressed against her side. She pushed him away when he got too close. "I'm fine, butthead. Go check on Gregor and Bloop."

"Dad!" Sax ran to Gregor. He lay with his head in Ma's lap.

"I'm on it." Meggie pushed her way through to Gregor and knelt at his side. She held her left hand out and scanned his injuries. "Two shots to the chest, but they've missed his major organs. I'll make it okay, Sax."

She ripped through his shirt, then used her right hand to release anti-bacterial healer over the two wounds. She injected him with a painkiller, then finished bandaging him up.

"That should hold him until we get him to the Medical Center and get some blood into him."

"Thanks, Meggie." Sax stroked her dad's head.

Meggie hugged her, then moved to Nala. "Let me see it, lady."

Nala growled, but obeyed.

Ninetta sat on the ground beside Gregor. "He saved me. I fell and one of the assholes was about to shoot me. He jumped right in front of me."

"Gregor's a good guy," Beck said, looking Ma over. Luckily, she hadn't been injured. "Where's Bloop?"

"He's here." Pris and Darya were both crying.

Otto stood beside her and rocked the baby while

Pris stroked Bloop's furry head. He lay across her lap, whining softly.

Pris's Fyrling, Siri, lay against him, chirping softly.

"I set Darya down in his carrier while we worked. When they attacked, Bloop jumped into the carrier and lay over him."

"Some asshole tried to shoot the baby," Icarus said, expression tortured. "I killed him, but he hit Bloop."

Beck fell to his knees beside her and stroked Bloop's cold nose. His droids circled above them, waiting for orders. He wanted to fucking kill the people who hurt his sister and his friends, but he knew they already lay dead.

"Dr. Bloop." Meggie knelt beside him. "Don't you worry, pupper. I've got you." She scanned him. "It looks like a graze, but he's a little guy. It hurts, doesn't it, buddy?" She applied a small amount of micro-healer to the wound before bandaging it up.

"That shot would have killed, Darya." Pris sobbed. "Dr. Bloop, I'm going to feed you steak every night. Okay?"

Beol deactivated his shield, and Beck wrapped his arms around his mate's legs. "Who were they? They were a lot better fighters than the Concords."

"The Equinox Guild." Bendix scowled and held up the hand of one of the attackers. The man had a black tattoo of a sun.

"They're another assassin guild." Beol kicked one of the bodies. "They aren't especially good, but they aren't the worst."

"They're a knock-off version of Half-Moon,"

Ninetta said. "They hate us too. Look at that one, Guild Master." She pointed to one of the bodies. "I recognized the way he moved. It's Bayne."

Beol pulled the man's mask off and swore. "That fucker. No wonder they got in so easily."

"They only tripped the sensors Gregor helped set up yesterday," Bendix said.

A shuttle pulled up and medics poured out of it, along with Renee Juren, the station's Security Chief.

"Fasi's on his way," she said, striding toward them. She stopped when she saw the tattooed hand Bendix held up and waved at her. "How the hell did this many assassins get into the station?"

"I have Finn working on it." Hack limped over. "Damn, they were tougher than the Concords. I've gotten lazy."

Beck focused, and his bot flew to Hack and let loose a spray of bubbles over his friend's head.

Hack glared at him. "Yeah. I'm glad you're alive too, Beck. Is my grandpuppy alright?"

Pris sniffled. "He's a hero."

Medics loaded Gregor and Nala onto stretchers and carried them to the shuttle. Fortunately, only one other Half-Moon member was badly injured. The shuttle sped away, carrying them to the Medical Center.

Ma hugged Sax. "I'm going to go and keep track of my girl and your pa, sweetheart. You need to stay here where it's safer."

Selene took Sax's hand. "He'll be alright. Meggie said so."

Sax gave Ma a sad look. "Will you update me?"

"Of course." Ma kissed her head.

"I'll go with you," Becca said. The two women hurried toward the tram.

"Bayne was a former member of Half-Moon. He was one of the few who left when I killed the old Guild Master," Beol said. "He knew our security well. I really don't regret not letting him take any of our tech with him when he left."

"That doesn't explain how so many of them could get onto the station." Renee frowned. "We have protocols in place, and security is tight right now because of the Council's worry over HF."

"Oh, fuck." Hack winced as he looked at his comm. "Finn and Lucas managed to trace their entry. They were given special permission."

"Who the fuck would do that?" Renee looked furious.

———

"Those disgusting creatures can't become citizens of Charybdis Station. They're unnatural and soulless robots. All that we've built here will be ruined."

They all gathered in one of Fasi's conference rooms with the Council and most of Half-Moon and Blue Solace.

Councilwoman Brinanda paced in front of them.

"Brinanda, why? Why didn't you just say something during the meeting?" Delino and the others looked shocked.

She stopped pacing and glared at them all.

"Seriously? Say something against Fasi's pet engineer? You all went along with it like the sheep you are. You've gone along with every single idea of his."

"Because they're good ideas, damn it." Councilwoman Rundel stood. "If you had a problem with any of it, then you were supposed to bring your concerns to us, not keep quiet and hire assassins to attack our own people."

"What good would it do? You all follow him blindly." Brinanda sneered at them all. "Charybdis Station could be magnificent; instead, we're fighting a war against ancient beings and taking in every refugee that comes along."

"Three people were badly injured, Brinanda, and a baby was almost killed," Delino said, voice harsh.

Hack looked up from his comm. "Let's be honest here, Brinanda. You say you care so much for Charybdis Station. That's your motive, right? Explain why you ordered them to *kidnap* one of the Bracken?"

"Kidnap? I thought they were trying to kill Icarus?" Mitchell leaned back, looking at Beck's son. "They weren't trying to kill you?"

"No," Icarus said, eyes coldly fixed on Brinanda. "They were trying to kill the others, but they kept trying to grab me. It made the fuckers much easier to kill."

"Gregor woke up a few minutes ago and checked his tablet," Hack said. "He secured the files they sent to you all, and he got an alert saying you sent everything to a corporation on Rueal. Draif is looking into your accounts now. Fortunately, Gregor's little tracker corrupted the files as soon as they were sent."

Brinanda paled.

"Oh, Brinanda," Jalina said, voice disgusted. "You betrayed our home for credits?"

Beck grabbed Icarus's hand and left the conference room. His heart was sick.

10

ONE MONTH LATER

*B*eol leaned over the toilet and emptied his stomach for the third time that morning. Tinker sat on the counter and chittered nervously, wringing her hands.

Dr. Bloop leaned up and licked his neck in concern. The puppy was almost fully recuperated from his injuries a month ago and was back to being his normal, bossy self.

"Woof."

"No, Bloop. I'm not sure that I'm pregnant. I don't want to get Beck's hopes up for nothing. He's been so sad lately."

"Woof."

"I know I can go ask Meggie or Becca for help. I just… need to think on things a little longer."

"Woof."

"Don't tell me what to do, puppy! I know I still haven't told Beck I love him."

A warm hand on his back made him turn his head. Wolfe crouched beside him, worry covering his face.

Leti stood in the doorway. "Are you talking to Bloop?"

"Maybe."

"Does he talk back?"

"Maybe."

Leti grinned. "Just making sure. Be right back."

He darted away.

Wolfe grabbed Beol's chin to get his attention and signed. "You're sick again. This is the seventh time you've been late to training this month."

"Only four of those have been because I'm sick."

"Ah, the joys of mated bliss," Wolfe signed.

Wolfe might have been joking, but Beol knew it was the plain and honest truth. Waking up every morning with Beck was the most beautiful experience of his life. His big mate's snores were as loud as a freight carrier, Dr. Bloop's were almost as bad, but Beol wouldn't change a single thing.

"Please call Meggie," Wolfe signed. "You need to have her check you out."

"I'll be alright. Why did you let Leti in the house?"

"Beck gave him your password. Blame him." Wolfe frowned. "You're lucky I haven't told Beck or Ma about you being sick. They would be all over you with worry."

"Beck doesn't need this right now. He's still upset about Brinanda."

Wolfe scowled. "The bitch should have been executed."

"That's not how Charybdis Station works."

The Council had decided she would be removed from the Council and exiled from Charybdis Station for her abuse of power. Their only problem was she had been privy to their planning sessions concerning HF. Fasi had decided she would be imprisoned until her knowledge was no longer relevant.

It really would have been nice to see her executed. Beol was the one who had to watch Beck struggle to trust his home station again.

"Knock, knock." Meggie poked her head into the bathroom. "I hear someone has a tummy ache."

"I'm not five, Meggie."

"Could have fooled me. You're acting like a pouting child." She grinned and knelt beside him, pulling Bloop into her arms.

Leti leaned inside. "Don't kill me, okay? I'm your best friend, and I just want to make sure you're not dying."

Wolfe's eyes danced with laughter, and he patted Beol's back.

"I'm not dying. I just have a stomach bug or something."

"If I don't think about it, it'll go away," Meggie said, deepening her voice to mock him. "I'm the big, bad assassin king. I can't show weakness." She held her hand up and quickly scanned him. Her eyes widened. "Oh, fuck."

Beol struggled to straighten up with Wolfe's help, but his stomach rolled again. "What's wrong?"

"Is he really dying?" Wolfe looked frightened.

Tinker flew around them, squawking with agitation.

"Oh, no." Meggie shook her head furiously. "No, he's not dying." She was quiet, avoiding their eyes as she looked around the room. "I'm glad I don't digest food."

"Meggie," Leti said, voice high. "Spit it out already."

She turned back to Beol and forced a smile. "Congratulations! You're pregnant."

"Why are your eyes telling us you have bad news, but your words are good news?" Wolfe signed.

"Pregnant isn't really *good* news, Wolfe," Beol said, pale. Icarus was easy to love, but babies were a different story.

"It's the absolute *best* news, grumpy kitty," Leti said. "You'll be a good daddy, don't you worry. Now, Meggie, why do you look like you want to throw up? You don't digest food, remember?"

"It's twins."

Beol's stomach rolled and he leaned over the toilet again, gagging.

Leti squealed and did a little dance in the doorway.

Meggie winced. "My scan analyzes DNA as well. Would you like to know the gender and genetic make-up of each baby?"

"Your scan does that?" Beol leaned back against Wolfe and let his brother press a wet cloth to his head.

Meggie nodded and spread her hands wide, dramatically framing her face. "Mom had *ideas* when they designed me."

"What can you tell us?" Wolfe looked completely

dumbfounded, and normally, Beol would have found that hilarious. Unfortunately, he was shell-shocked himself.

"Two boys. One has more of your genetics while the other will be a hell of a lot like Beck. You're just over a month along, and the babies are doing just fine."

"Fuck."

"At least, I think they are. I'm not really a doctor, you know."

"Wow. We feel so much better now, Meggie," Wolfe signed and gave her a dry look.

"You need to work on your bedside manner," Leti added.

She ignored them and patted Beol's head. "You, however, are dehydrated and need food to stay in your belly. Poor, grumpy kitty." She injected him with something. "This will help your nausea, and then we can get some fluids in you."

"Twins," he repeated, completely drained. "Two boys."

"Beck told us he wants a bunch of kids." Meggie grinned again. "This is a good start."

"Meggie, you're wonderful, but your smile makes me want to cut you."

She rocked back on her heels, cackling like a hyena.

"What's going on in here? Beol, sweetie, are you alright?" Ma stood behind Leti in the doorway, looking them over. "Meggie, love, what is wrong with you?"

"I've asked myself that same question several times the past ten minutes." Beol groaned as Wolfe helped him to his feet. "Ma, I need you."

The large yellow Grell smiled wide.

In moments, Leti, Wolfe, Meggie, and Bloop were out the door, the toilet was flushed, his face was washed, and he was in the process of brushing his teeth.

When he finished, Ma pulled him into her soft arms, and he rested his head against her ample chest. "What's wrong, sweetheart?"

"Beck is still upset about Brinanda. I'm scared to tell him I love him. It's hard to trust people because my mom was a fucking asshole. It's my fault Icarus almost got taken and Bloop, Nala, and Gregor were hurt. I feel like shit, and I'm pregnant with twins."

Ma's mouth hung open. She shook her head and took a deep breath, slowly letting it out.

"There's a lot running through your head, isn't there?"

"So much." He sighed.

"Now, I know the Brinanda thing shook us all up. Beck just has to process his own feelings, just like everyone has had to. He'll get there."

"I don't like seeing him upset."

"He's been lucky in family and friends his whole life. Betrayal hurts. He still has us though. Doesn't he?"

"Yes," Beol said, rubbing his face against her shoulder.

"As for you, sweetie, you trusted me enough to tell me all of this. I think you're learning there are a lot of people around you that love and respect you. Give it time. Honestly though, you already *do* trust my Beckie Boo. You've moved him into your home, share his bed, and accept his son as your own. You trust him with your brother and your guild members. Now, you need to trust him with your heart. You know he already has it, so what will saying the words actually change?"

Beol closed his eyes and soaked up her affection. She *was* right. Beck had already invaded his heart and home. There was no going back, and he didn't regret it.

His home was so much warmer with Beck and Icarus there. Then there was Bloop and Tinker. The two brightened his day, just by existing.

"Okay. I can do it. I'll tell him I love him."

Ma stroked his hair. "Good, sweetheart. Now, tell me about your mother."

Surprisingly, the words practically flew out of his mouth.

"I adored her when I was little. She would read me bedtime stories and spend time with me. My father barely looked at me, little less spoke to me, but Mom seemed to love me."

"What happened?"

"When I was about six, I met this nice woman named Lolita. She had a shop in our neighborhood. Every time I went in, she would sit me down and feed me this bread. What did she call it? Oh, yeah. Bredell honey bread. Anyway, she had this big fluffy cat, and I would sneak away from home and go visit all the time. I'd sit and pet Moodle and eat bread."

"Why did you have to sneak? I would think your mother would like Lolita."

"I was homeschooled so I could be properly trained. Father didn't like me to be around strangers."

"Oh dear. What happened to Lolita?"

"One day, I brought some of the bread home with me. That night, I threw a fit and demanded to go to school like a normal person. My father was pissed, but Mom calmed him down and put me to bed. She said she'd talk to him, and I was so happy. I gave her my bread and told her about Lolita.

"The next day, Mom took me to the store, but Lolita wasn't there. It was closed. One of her grandsons was there to pick up Moodle. He told us Lolita had been murdered, and the store was closing. Mom acted so sad, but when we got to the house, she sat me down and asked why I didn't tell her about the cat. I was so confused. Why would that matter?"

Ma kissed his cheek and wiped the tears from his face.

"Mom told me that I would train with Father and that I wouldn't complain, or she would go back for the cat and kill him like she did Lolita. I knew then. She was even worse than him. She could make you love her, then smile as she tore your heart out."

"Is she dead?"

"Yeah. She died during a mission. I think Hay was in love with her. He worshiped the ground she walked on, but after Wolfe was born, she became more blatant. He was shocked by how she treated us.

"He's always been there for Wolfe and me, and I thought it was for her, you know? Then they went on a mission together and she died. He didn't seem that upset, and I always wondered what happened. *If* anything happened."

"I'm glad she's dead, and if Hay had a hand in it, all the better." Her arms tightened. "No one hurts my babies."

"Ma, I'm not your baby. I know I'm Beck's mate, but you don't have to act."

He tried to pull away. Damn, he was embarrassed. Here he was, spilling his heart all over the poor woman.

Ma growled. "Don't be an idiot, Beol." She looked down into his eyes. "Do you know when you became mine?"

"When Beck met me."

"No. When I met Pris and little Darya." Ma cupped his face. "She told me all about her beloved Guild Master and how he stepped up and killed his father because he wanted her and Otto to have the chance to raise Darya in peace."

"Ma."

"I knew then that you belonged to me and Pops. I know it's hard to accept love. I see you struggle with loving Wolfe and you two are brothers. Soon enough, you'll figure out that the people around you are your family, and we will be there for you until the day we die."

He buried his face against her shoulder. This woman gave seriously good hugs. "Love is the most frightening thing I've ever felt."

"Nothing hurts worse than a broken heart, but trust me, it's worth the risk. Even if it were to just last seconds, it's worth the risk." She set him back and shook his shoulders. "You'll tell Beck you love him when it feels right to you. Now, what's this nonsense about that whole Equinox attack being your fault?"

"I was supposed to protect Icarus and the others. It's my responsibility."

"You did protect them. You're overthinking it, sweetie pie."

Beol shook his head. "Did you see Beck? He saved the day."

Ma laughed, and her whole body shook. "My boy sure likes his toys, but Beol, you were there fighting too. Do you really need to be the flashy hero to feel like you got the job done?"

He winced. "Am I really being that arrogant?"

"It happens to most men one time or another."

He laughed, voice hoarse. "Okay. Are you even going to mention the twins?"

"I'm still wrapping my head around that one, sweetheart. My mama and grandmamma both had a set of twins, so I don't know why I'm so surprised."

"Ma, do you have Beol in there with you?" Beck's voice came through the door.

"We're having a moment. Leave us alone," she yelled back.

"In the bathroom? There's a whole house out here."

"Oh, go make a glitter bot or something, son. You're ruining our moment."

"Hmm, that's a really good idea. Bloop and I will be in the workshop if you need us, Beol."

Beol laughed against Ma's shoulder. "I really do love that man."

A few minutes and a few tears later, Beol sat at the kitchen table.

"Here's a nice bowl of soup, Dad." Icarus set a steaming bowl in front of him, then leaned down and gently hugged him. "I can't believe I'm going to be a big brother. I'm going to take such good care of you and the babies."

Beol took a bite and enjoyed the warmth settling in his belly. Two years ago, he never would have imagined he would have a mate, a son, and two babies on the way. Change happened fast, but he was adaptable. It had saved his life more than once, and now, it would help him enjoy that life.

*B*eck growled as another request came through his comm. "I swear, Bloop, if I had known *everyone* would want to have a neuro-control implant, I wouldn't have invented it."

"Woof."

"Okay, okay. I definitely would have, but I would have made it seem like it was a lot harder to make. That would have made them think twice. Right?"

"Woof."

"I agree, Bloop. Beck is just being a big baby," Gregor said as he walked into the workshop.

Beck looked up from his workstation. It was unusual to see the man without Ninetta. The two had become inseparable since the attack from Equinox. Beck had the feeling it was more than just gratefulness on Ninetta's part.

"Hey. How are you feeling?"

Beck's friend sat, panting a bit from the walk. "I'm

getting better every day, but I miss my girl. Selene stole Sax from me."

Beck snorted. "Sorry, man. Selene has a mind of her own. You know she stole over half Beol's weapons, right? He's never getting those back."

Gregor smiled and shook his head. "She makes a good mentor though."

"She does." Beck nodded. "She makes a good mother too. Rus adores her and Xu, both." Beck watched him from the corner of his eye. "What's wrong, Gregor? You're acting all squirrelly."

"Do you think Ninetta only likes me because I got shot helping her?"

"No." Beck shook his head. "Honestly, I think you caught her eye because you got shot helping her. Now? Now, she really likes you. She got to know you, and I can see she's smitten. Clear as day."

"Smitten?" Gregor smiled. "I love your way with words, man."

"How do you feel about Ninetta?"

Gregor rolled his eyes. "I'm *smitten*. How could I not be? The woman is amazing. I wish humans could somehow tell if someone was their life-mate or soulmate, whatever you want to call it."

"I have to admit, it helped knowing right away that Beol was mine. It gave me the little bit of courage I had to court him."

Beck's comm chimed, and he looked at it. "Uh oh. Hack says we need to meet at his house."

"The Queen and HF?"

"Probably. They've been quiet the last few weeks, but that can't last long."

"I'll stay here with Icarus."

Beck sighed. "Thank you. I know I'm being crazy. I haven't let him leave the house without a guard or stay home by himself since the attack. That's not fair to him, but I can't seem to help it."

"He understands, and it'll get better, Beck. Soon the Council will finish determining their sentience and take the vote about citizenship."

"Beck?" Beol came into the workshop. Beck's mate looked pale and tired.

"Are you alright?" Beck rushed to him and cupped his face in his hands. "You don't feel warm. Do you need some soup? I'll call Ma. She'll know what to do."

Beol closed his eyes and gripped Beck's wrists. He pressed his cheek into Beck's hand and practically purred. "I'm fine. Don't move. I love it when you touch me."

"Uh, should I leave?"

Beol didn't even open his eyes. "Don't bother. We have to go see fucking Hack. Would you mind staying with Icarus?"

Gregor grinned. "I planned on it. You two are good dads."

Beol smiled and leaned into Beck. "Ninetta's on her way too. She's enjoying her new leg."

Gregor blushed.

"Don't make out on our couch," Icarus said from the door. "That's my dads' spot."

Beck shared a grin with his son. They were both hoping Gregor and Ninetta became a couple.

"I'll make dinner while you're gone. Juniper's coming over to show me a new recipe."

Beol finally opened his eyes. "You have your extra shields, phasers, and vibro-blades?"

"Yes." Icarus nodded. Beck knew Icarus wasn't afraid to jump in and protect the ones he loved, and that made him even more nervous.

"We'll be back soon hopefully." Beck tugged on his mate, and they left the workshop.

Bloop met them at the door with his leash in his mouth, and Tinker perched on his head.

"I guess these two are coming with." Beck snapped Bloop's leash on, and Tinker flew to Beol's shoulder.

They opened the door to find Sax, Becca, and Meggie whispering to one another. They all looked up, startled.

"Oh. Hi, Beol." Becca swallowed and looked straight at his belly. "Have you spoken to Beck yet?"

Beck looked questioningly at his mate.

Beol sighed. "Not yet. I'll tell him on the way home."

"We're going to stay with Icarus until you get back." Sax pushed by them, then looked over her shoulder. "Oh, I told Selene already. You should tell Beck on the way to the meeting."

"Meggie, did you have to tell everyone?" Beol glared at the woman.

"Yes." She nodded and grinned. "I really did."

"Okay? What's going on?" Beck was starting to

worry. Despite keeping Icarus and the girls a secret for so long, he really didn't like secrets being kept from him.

"Come on." Beol took his hand, and they walked toward the tram.

He was silent for a moment. They let Bloop sniff around one of Rus's freshly planted flowers, while Tinker chirped softly in Beol's ear.

"I love you, Beck."

Beck froze and a grin slowly covered his face. It felt like he had waited years to hear those words instead of a couple of months.

Beck picked his mate up and hugged him tight, Beol's feet dangling off the ground. "I love you so much, Beol. We're mates now, right? Can we get married?"

Beol wrapped his arms around Beck's neck and buried his face against Beck's neck. "Anything you want. As long as I'm with you, I'll be happy."

"You two going to make it to Hack's house?" Bendix and his Fyrling stopped to watch them.

Bendix had named the small hippogriff Fyrling Murphy, and Beck was surprised how similar the two were to one another. They were both snarky, tough, and a tad bit arrogant.

"We're going," Beol finally answered him.

"Are you sure? You guys should be celebrating. I mean, come on, boss man. Twins? That's awesome."

"Twins?"

Beol's guilty wince told Beck he hadn't misheard,

and he felt lightheaded. Black spots danced around him, then he fell.

Beck woke up slowly. Beol's voice sounded worried, but Meggie was reassuring him. Why was he lying down?

He remembered suddenly, and his eyes popped open. "Beol? We're having twins?"

Beol bent over him, concerned. "Are you alright, Sparky? You went down hard."

"Twins?"

Beol gave him a nervous smile. "I just found out."

Beck sat up and hugged Beol, pulling him into his lap. "I can't even find the words, Beol. I've always wanted kids."

"Now we'll have three." Beol stroked his cheek.

Icarus crouched beside them. "I'll be a good big brother, Dad. Xu says I'm great."

"So," Bendix said slowly. "Go home and celebrate. I'll let you all know what Hack says."

"No. I'm okay." Beck grinned. "I'm really, really okay."

Beol arched a brow. "You want to tell everyone, don't you?"

Beck nodded enthusiastically.

"Come on, Sparky. Let's get moving." Beol helped him up.

Beck picked Beol up and headed for the tram.

"Uh, why are you carrying me?"

"You weren't feeling good earlier."

"I'm alright now."

Beck nuzzled his neck. "I like carrying you."

They got on the tram, and Beol smacked Beck's chest. "I'm not being carried into a meeting with Hack."

Beck groaned but set Beol down. "It's not a meeting if it's at Hack's house."

"It's a meeting."

They arrived at Hack and Leti's, and Beck's happiness started to fade. They gathered in the backyard like usual, but there were too many grim faces. Leti sat beside Hack, looking furious and close to tears. The older kids were in school, and the yard looked oddly empty without them running around, adding more tension to the atmosphere.

Beck found a seat next to Selene and squeezed Beol's hand tightly. Something was definitely wrong. Bloop pressed against his leg, and Tinker cuddled into Beol's neck.

Fasi stood, Pepper perched on his hip. He cleared his throat. "Thanks for coming. We have some news, but we need to keep this all as under the radar as we can."

Beol narrowed his eyes. "Why the secrecy?"

Renee stood from her seat, pulling their attention to her. Fasi's wife went to stand next to her husband and grabbed his hand.

"Recently, we found out that, immediately after our conversation with Beck and his friends about the Bracken, Brinanda was contacted about selling the information. We thought she reached out to the buyer, but that wasn't the case. Draif did some digging, and the buyer works for a company owned by a member of HF."

"They have eyes on us?" Beck frowned. "Enforcement scans the conference rooms for bugs every day."

"I've checked, and as far as I can tell, they're doing their jobs," Renee said. "We believe it's someone on Fasi's staff. Until we find out, we'll meet here for strategy planning."

"Don't stop all meetings," Beol warned. "They'll know you're onto them."

Fasi nodded. "We'll continue having the lovely, mundane weekly Council meetings there."

"I challenge them not to fall asleep during the budget meeting," Councilman Mitchell said.

Fasi snorted. "That's the truth. Okay, now. After weeks of debating what to do about the Queen and HF, we've come to a decision. HF isn't stopping, and their actions are having an effect on the galaxy."

Draif stood. "The coalition has several high-powered members, but it's led by four very wealthy, very powerful people. I still don't understand why the Queen serves them, but it can't be a coincidence that every single planet that has been destroyed has boosted these four individuals' profit lines."

Bendix looked disgusted. "Seriously? That's why they're really doing this?"

"Bredell was Air's first known victim," Fasi said. "From what Draif has found, HF's leadership had three major competitors that were on vacation at Bredell when it was destroyed. All three were killed."

"Two more major competitors were vacationing on Dairilve when Air destroyed it," Draif added. "With their deaths, HF's business interests made a lot of credits taking over their customers and resources."

"Gods," Beck said, feeling sick. "All those people dead for credits."

"Icewilde was a major industrial world. One of the four, Cortez, practically owns his own industrial world, and Icewilde was his main competitor," Fasi said.

Beol patted his hand. "What about Union Station?"

Draif winced. "They had a poor relationship with Vextonar. Cortez and one of the other three primarily live on Vextonar. They both do a lot of business from there."

Leti growled. "Fucking Cortez."

Beck exchanged looks with the others. Who the fuck was Cortez, and why was Leti pissed off at him? Leti actually sounded slightly fierce.

"Elusa was full of powerful celebrities that were also activists," Draif added, shaking his head. "Ava and I are pushing the media to cover HF's actions, but it's getting more difficult. They're scared."

"It all makes a horrible kind of sense," Fasi said, "HF's motives are clear. Their connection to the Queen and her Elements is not. We know they work together, but not the dynamics."

"Since HF publicly acknowledged their alliance with the Queen, their profits have shot down. Even with less competition, their customers are going elsewhere," Draif said. "Unsurprisingly, people aren't happy with them. There are very few pure humans anymore, but even most of those who would fall under HF's idea of *superior* don't support them. The Galactic Economy is going crazy."

Councilman Delino nodded. "We expected the economic fallout, and we're taking measures to balance what we can. What we didn't fully anticipate was how the other systems would react."

"In response to the destruction of Union Station as well as all the planets Air attacked, *two* planets have exiled all non-native species," Fasi said.

Beck frowned, concerned. The galaxy was interdependent and a mishmash of species. If they started to separate and isolate themselves from everyone else, it would lead to a lot of chaos.

"Why would they do that?" Dru asked.

"Fear," Ava answered. Hack's diplomacy officer sighed. "Charybdis Station has always been a mix of species, so it's hard for us to understand, but Siletus and Dramacus only recently accepted non-native citizens. Seeing HF target any and all non-human species has made many pull into themselves. They feel they can only trust their own species. I'm afraid we'll see more of this if HF isn't defeated."

"They aren't just a physical threat," Hack said, sighing. "I hate this bullshit. How do you fight that?"

"The first step is in taking away their most powerful weapon," Fasi said. "For their own benefit, HF has ordered the deaths of billions of people. Without the Crellic Queen and her Elements, destroying a planet isn't an easy thing to do. It takes manpower and a hell of a lot of fighting. The Queen needs to go."

"What's the plan?" Audre, the Yellow General, crossed her arms and leaned back in her chair.

"Divide and conquer," Fasi said. "We fight HF behind the scenes while we take the Queen out of commission. Beol's scouts have reported the Queen and Earth are both on Genarg. The planet has become a hub of mercenaries and other hired fighters, all under the command of HF."

"Is that their base?" Dru asked. "We could remove the threat completely by taking that world."

"Unfortunately, it's not," Draif answered. "I've been following their movements closely and most of their forces are spread across the galaxy. Their leadership is split between Vextonar and Rueal." He looked thoughtful. "However, if their goal truly is to establish human dominance in the galaxy, it won't be long until they start establishing bases. Leti's university friends are worried that Vextonar will become the first one. Dottie noticed a lot of humans pouring in through the spaceports."

Leti wiped his eyes. "My friend, Advaith, says the Prime on Vextonar have recently passed laws censoring higher education. That's when he started paying attention to what they were doing. They already hold the government and military. He says their recent political rants sound a lot like HF. Fasi said he could move here with his family, and he's actually considering it. He's afraid."

"This is why we have to divide and conquer," Fasi

said, bouncing Pepper on his hip. "If we focus only on HF, the Queen will kill more people. If we only focus on the Queen, then HF strengthens their hold on the galaxy. I fear we were too focused on the Elements and the Concords over the last year."

"We missed the early signs of HF, and fuck, but we still don't understand their connection to the Queen. They seem to control her, but can she really even be controlled?" Draif said, shaking his head. "The galaxy was successfully distracted while they set things up, that's for sure."

"This cycle is so different from any that have come before," Death said. "I can't offer any insight into her actions."

"What we *do* know right now is that HF has made sure the Queen is protected," Renee said. "Beol's scouts have managed to get close and have sent us video. She's there."

"We're taking the Queen out first, then?" Dru looked eager. "I'm ready for this shit to be over."

"An outright attack isn't the right strategy here." Fasi shook his head. "For one, it would take a good chunk of our forces to do it, and HF's leadership would likely jump on the chance to attack the station while we're vulnerable. Also, even with Fire and Death's help, the Queen will likely be difficult to kill if she sees us coming."

"We're thinking of a more indirect approach," Renee said. "We can think of no easy way to destroy the Queen. Death can't take her soul, she can see through our new shields, and she will heal too quickly from damage that would kill anyone else. Killing her at a distance is out too. A shot to the head won't do the job."

"We thought of trying to simply destroy the planet, but we're a little short of insane and cruel Elements. Our best chance is subtlety," Fasi said. "We plan on sending a small fleet of five ships, to the planet. That few should be able to remain undetected."

Cas, the Green General, leaned forward. "They would sneak onto the planet and kill the Queen and Earth?"

"That's the plan," Renee said. "We've already asked Hack to lead them. He works well with Death and Fire and has been a part of this from the start."

Beck bit his lip. That definitely explained why Leti looked so upset. That also meant that Beck would be leaving his pregnant mate behind, and he didn't like that one bit. He had a responsibility to the station though, and he would honor that.

"Ideally, this small fleet would remove the Queen and Earth from HF's repertoire of weapons," Fasi said. "Then, we would focus on taking down their leadership."

Sheiria, the Red General, looked concerned. "How do we do that? They're powerful, wealthy, and protected by some of the best."

"Draif and Ava have a plan," Fasi said, eyes sparkling with intent. He exchanged grins with the two.

Beck knew Leti's best friend was damn smart, and Ava was sneaky. He kinda wanted to know what those two would do.

"HF will pay for all those they've killed. Don't

worry about that. For now, those remaining at the station will focus on defense. When the Queen dies, Charybdis Station will become more of a target than we already are."

Councilman Delino stood. "We've talked about it quite a bit, and we'd like our remaining generals to work together to protect Charybdis and the system. Lieutenant Finn will lead the Blue Fleet in Hack's absence."

Beck smiled encouragingly at Finn when the young cardinal turned green.

Fasi nodded in agreement. "Hack will leave on the Blue Solace in two days, accompanied by four ships of his choice. On record, he is going on a diplomatic mission to Burnished Outpost."

"Draif and Ava will begin the first stage of our *attack* on HF within the week. They're working with allies to sabotage the four leaders of HF's already faltering businesses," Delino said. "Credits are what drives them, and we plan to hit them hard."

"We'll update you all on both missions as things progress," Fasi said. "It's Hack's house, so there's food cooking. Feel free to stay and chat. We have a lot to do over the next few months, and there won't be much free time. Enjoy it while you can."

Fasi sat back down and cuddled Pepper. "Beol, Draif has something to ask you before you leave."

Selene pulled Beck from his chair. "Come on. We need to tell Hack about your twins. Beol can handle this without you."

Freed from his leash, Bloop ran over to visit his

parents, Peri and Gravy. Beck and Beol shared a smile when Bloop pounced on Gravy.

Beol nudged him with his foot. "She's right. Go share our news, Sparky."

Beck groaned and watched his smiling mate over his shoulder as his friend dragged him away.

eol thought over Draif's request. "Okay. I'll talk to Bendix, and you can work with him on it. I'll be going with Beck, so he'll be the one in charge here."

Draif grinned. "Thanks. It's moments like this that make me so damn happy you and your guild moved to Charybdis Station."

"We do appreciate it, Beol," Fasi said. He slung his arm around Beol's shoulders. "We appreciate the way you make our Beck smile even more."

Draif nodded. "So, I hear you're having twins? Fire and Meggie are pretty close, and she blabbed."

Beol sighed. "Meggie *is* the bigmouth."

Draif looked at him strangely. "Huh?"

Beol waved him away. "Nothing. Yes, I am pregnant, and it's twins. Lord Admiral, you stop messaging Ma right now. She already knows."

Fasi looked disappointed. "Does Pops know?"

"Probably."

"Damn it."

Draif snickered. "Come on. You might want to let Hack know you're going."

They worked their way through the crowd of people while Tinker sat on Beol's shoulder and chattered to Draif.

"She really is cute. I wish I knew what she was saying."

Beol snorted. "Trust me. She has ways of letting you know what she wants." Beol paused as he walked past Bendix. "Hey, Draif needs to talk to you. He has plans, and I fully approve. You'll be in charge while I'm gone on this crazy-ass mission."

Bendix grinned and shrugged. "Okay, but you know I'll approve Moyra's request to have a bubble bot patrol the neighborhood."

Beol sighed. "Do what you must."

He looked around but couldn't find Beck, so he headed inside. The place was full, and Ma, Icarus, and Juniper were cooking in the kitchen.

"Rus? What are you doing here?"

"Dad." Icarus leaned down and kissed his cheek. "Sebastian and Fire came over and told us something important was happening. I wanted to help Ma and Juny cook dinner so you all can sit and talk. Noe and Wolfe brought all of us over, so I was protected. I promise."

"I'm glad you're here, Rus." Beol smiled reassuringly. Icarus reminded him so much of Beck – all earnest and sweet.

Ma hugged him from behind. "Hey, sweetheart.

Beck is in the living room."

Beol let himself sink against her for a moment, then pushed away. "Thanks, Ma."

The living room was full of people and pets. His mate sat on a large pillow seat with Sami and Milo in his lap. Wolfe lounged on the floor next to him, a large Betonize hunting cat sprawled across his lap. Sami's cat had taken a liking to Wolfe, and Beol knew his brother wanted one of his own.

Beck grinned at him and scooted over so Beol could sit next to him.

Hack and Selene sat across from them on their own pillows, and Leti curled up against Hack, face buried in his chest.

"Haroon, Dru, and Xav will come with me. Do you think we'll have any other volunteers?"

Beol snorted. "All of your captains would volunteer, but we need to stay discreet if possible. You're the Blue General. They practically worship you and Leti, and they'd make a huge deal out of going with you."

Hack looked surprised, then grinned. "Really?"

"Yes, really. When they find out, they'll be upset you're borrowing Xavier from the Yellow General."

Hack sighed. "I still need to pick one more."

"No, you don't. If she's willing, Moyra will captain the fifth ship, and I'll be on yours," Beol said firmly. "I go where my mate goes."

"Yes!" Moyra jumped up and danced around the chair Noe sat in. "I'm the first assassin captain of Charybdis Station. In your face, Noe!"

Noe looked disgruntled. "I suppose I'd best go with you to make sure you don't blow yourself up."

Wolfe clapped, then signed. "I get to be her assassin lieutenant."

"Stop putting assassin in front of everything," Beol grumbled. "It's just for the mission. Don't let the power go to your head, Moyra."

Moyra smirked. "Too late. Noe, drop and give me fifty. You need to stay in shape if you're going to be my assassin soldier."

Noe arched a brow. "Yeah. I'll get right on that, Captain."

"Beol," Beck hissed. "You're in a delicate condition right now."

Beol raised his brow. "So is Sebastian, but he has to go. I'll handle it, Sparky. This isn't up for negotiation."

Beck narrowed his eyes and growled.

"I think now is a good time to let you know, Will, that I'm going too," Leti said, sitting up and crossing his arms. "Renee and Fasi have already agreed to help Grandpa Moses watch the kids, and Ma and Pops will be next door with Sebastian's bunch."

"Hell no," Hack said, shaking his head.

Leti arched his brow perfectly. "This isn't up for negotiation."

"Damn it, Beol." Hack glared at him.

Beol shrugged. "Don't blame me."

Sebastian groaned. He sat smooshed between Fire and Alois on one of the loveseats. "Hack, I hate saying this, I really do, but Leti knows a lot about the Crellic System. I can translate, but he's the one that puts the puzzles together. We don't know what we're facing on Genarg, and we'll need every resource."

"What about the kids, Leti?" Hack asked, voice breaking. "It will take at least three months to get there, then get home. It'll be even worse with both of us gone."

Leti slumped. "I know. I hate the thought of leaving them for even a day, little less months, but I have to do this too, Hack. If the Queen survives, she will come after the station. I don't know how much help I'll be, but even if it's a little bit, it's worth it to protect them."

The two men wrapped their arms around each other, and Beol's heart hurt for them. They loved their family so much, but Leti was right. They had to end this now before the Queen and HF made a move toward the station.

"I can't be too mad at you now," Beck said, wrapping an arm around him. "If Leti has to leave his kids behind to do this, then I can handle my very well-trained, badass, pregnant mate coming with. I didn't much want to leave you behind anyway."

Delino and the other Council members filed into the living room with Fasi.

The Lord Admiral put Pepper in the large playpen in the corner and took a seat next to his wife. He grinned at Beck and Beol. "We have *some* good news for today."

Delino sat beside Becca on the couch and smiled widely. "With the help of Dr. Morrick and Dr. Manning, the Council has formally determined what we already knew. The Bracken and the Charybdis

Fyrlings are both sentient. We'll make the official announcement next week."

Meggie squealed and clapped her hands. "I'm going to the Trade Market tomorrow. I have shopping to do."

"Meggie," Sax said, gently nudging her friend. "Everyone knowing we're sentient doesn't matter unless it comes with citizenship."

Meggie slumped. "Damn it."

Mitchell gave her a sympathetic look. "You really won't like what I'm going to suggest, Meggie."

Beol frowned. "What's your suggestion?"

"We need to elect a new Council member to replace Brinanda before we vote on citizenship."

"That could take months," Beck protested.

Beol pulled Beck's tail out of his hand and linked his fingers with his mate's.

"It could," Mitchell agreed. "That's why I suggest you take Meggie, Sax, and Icarus with you on the mission. You all will be traveling under the radar, and the only people who will know your exact location can be fully trusted."

"It would give us the time we need to elect a replacement and vote on your citizenship," Councilwoman Rundel said. The older Siren moaned as she arched her back. "Maybe we should replace me too. I'm getting too old for all this drama."

Fasi snorted. "You aren't leaving us, Rundel. I forbid it."

She gave him a look. "Don't get too big for your britches there, Lord Admiral. Anyway, we think it will be safer for you three, even if it means being confined to a small ship for months."

Meggie grinned. "I'm absolutely fine with that. I would love to be able to help Beck and Beol."

Sax nodded. "I'll fight for whoever will take me on as crew."

"She's mine," Hack yelled before Dru could say anything.

"Not fair." Dru scowled from her seat in her husband's lap. Her newt, Monty, sat on her head as usual.

"You took like half my crew with you," Hack said. "It's completely fair."

"You have Princess Buttercup!"

They all looked at Leti's Fire Veil Dragon. The large beast slept in the middle of the rug, puffs of smoke coming from his nose with each breath. Morgan's baby Frost Veil Dragon, Stardust, was curled on top of his head. Tiny bursts of ice and frost blew from his nose as he snored, just like Princess.

"I'm not convinced Princess is as valuable as we think he is," Hack said dryly.

"Will," Leti said with a gasp. "You take that back."

Hack winced. "Baby, I'm negotiating here."

Dru rolled her eyes. "If you get Sax and Beol, then I get Cordelia. You know she'll want to spend the trip with Quinn anyway."

"Fine, but I get Rune," Hack said. "Silas will be all weepy if he can't spend time with his man."

"Rus wants to go too," Sax said, smiling softly. "He already spoke to Juniper about going in his place to cook for the Blue Solace. Juniper said he'd transfer to Dru's ship to make sure they don't poison themselves."

"I don't know, Sax. You all are so young, and this would be your first mission." Beol frowned. "This won't be easy."

"No, it won't be." Sax met his gaze. "If we want Charybdis Station to accept us, then we need to prove our worth. That's not fair, but it's how it is. The Council and Fasi can stand behind us all they want, but if the average person sees us as outsiders, then that's what we'll always be."

"No," Leti said and stood, stomping over to Sax. "Charybdis Station has taken in so many, and you three are just like them."

He tried to hug Sax while standing, but tipped over, falling on top of her and Meggie.

Meggie and Sax both laughed and helped him straighten up.

"It's fine, Leti. We know we're different, but different doesn't mean worse or even better. We want to prove ourselves," Meggie said.

Beol huffed. He wanted to stay mad at Meggie for her loud-mouthed ways, but he was so damn proud of her and Sax.

Beck pulled him close, and suddenly, Beol found himself face to face with Sami. The little Betonize boy grinned at him, and Beol couldn't help but smile back. He covered his abdomen with his hand and sighed.

Tinker hummed against his neck, small body thrumming with excitement. Beol didn't know how much she understood, but she knew something was changing.

After eating and discussing their plans, Beol and his family finally made it home. Ninetta and Gregor were asleep on the couch.

"Why didn't they go back to Gregor's apartment?" Icarus looked at them over the back of the couch.

"Who knows? They look comfortable," Beck said, smiling. "We can let them sleep."

Later that night, Beol hung onto Beck's shoulders and pressed his face against his neck. Beck arched against him, dick filling Beol's ass.

"I love you so much, Beol."

Beol groaned when Beck hit just the right spot. "Love you too."

The words came easy, feeling as natural as their bodies moving together.

13

SILVERLIGHT SYSTEM, PLANET VEXTONAR - ONE MONTH LATER

Beck curled around his sleeping mate. He lay in bed and listened to the familiar sounds of the Blue Solace. Dr. Bloop snored from the bottom of the bed. He had gotten so much bigger in the past month that his pet bed was too small.

It was strange, but Beck had missed the ship so much. Everyone was close together, and the troubles of the galaxy had a way of seeming far away.

Their room was connected to the engineering bay and smelled like all his favorite things – Beol, oil, and metal. Icarus had hung some plants up for him, but otherwise, it was big, comfy used furniture and warm colors.

Tinker's new house sat under the porthole, adding a large spot of color to the room. Beck could see the little Fyrling moving around to check on her own tiny plants. Rus was a firm believer that every home needed plants.

Beck smiled and nuzzled Beol's neck.

"No," Beol said.

"What are you talking about?" Beck tried to sound innocent.

"You want to fuck again." Beol rolled over and buried his face against Beck's chest. "I'm too tired. Your damn kids drain me. Little fucking leeches."

Beck stroked his mate's back and made soothing sounds, even though he wanted to laugh. Beol wasn't handling pregnancy well. He was either nauseous or sleepy. There was no other state of being.

"Meggie says the second trimester should be a little easier."

Actually, she had said the second trimester came with new, fun adventures. Beck thought Beol might not need to hear that.

"It better be. I have a guild to run, and I still need to train."

"I'm sorry. I'd carry the babies if I could."

Beol scowled. "Fucking biology. These kids better be worth it."

Beck grinned. "Or what?"

Beol bit his shoulder. "Or they'll never have more siblings unless they're androids."

Dannol's voice came over the ship's comm. "We're docking in Vextonar now. Captain, uh, I mean General Hack wants everyone up and on guard."

Beol slowly sat up. "I'm going to check in with Wolfe and Noe. I need to make sure they haven't killed Moyra since we talked last time."

Beck laughed. Moyra was a bit crazy, but she made

a good captain, even if she was annoying and unpredictable.

"You mean, your visit isn't about checking up on your little brother?"

Beol pulled his clothes on and gave Beck a sheepish look. "Maybe a little bit. I'm getting used to him standing on his own two feet, but I miss the fucker. Are you getting up?"

"I'll be fueling up the ship." Beck sighed. "I like our home on the station, but I've gotta admit, I love our comfy love nest here."

"It's nice and private. That's for sure." Beol leaned over and kissed him. "Be careful, Sparky. Vextonar isn't a friendly planet anymore."

"As if it ever was," Beck grumbled, then climbed out of bed. The faster they got this done, the faster they could leave.

———

BECK FINISHED FUELING UP THE SHIP, FEELING DAMN antsy. Vextonar was crawling with Humans First soldiers. The only way they had managed to land without being detected was with Dottie's help. Their ship was docked in the far back of the spaceport and listed as a Drellian merchant ship.

The older woman stood beside him, as nervous as he was. She watched her tablet carefully, answering questions and keeping an eye on her port.

"Dottie, I've never seen you look this worried."

She looked up and rolled her shoulders. "I sent my family off planet."

"What? Your family's been here for over six generations."

"The Prime never liked me much, Beck, but now they scare me. You know me. I can't keep my mouth shut, and now I'm on their watch list."

"Watch list?" Beck shuddered.

"Truthfully, I've always been on it. They're just bolder now about saying it."

"You need to leave while you can, Dottie."

The woman shook her head. "I'm smuggling folks off planet every day. I won't leave people behind. Hell, I helped a bunch of Leti's university friends and their families leave just yesterday."

Beck frowned. "Why can't they just leave?"

"Vextonar isn't letting citizens leave without special permission."

"Why would they want people to stay if they don't want to be here?"

She looked around, then leaned close. "I have a friend that works for enforcement. From what I hear, they'll be rounding up all those that ain't *pure* enough to sell. They want to keep everyone here so they can make money off them."

Beck's eyes widened in horror. "Fuck, that's horrible. That can't be true."

"That's why I'm smuggling folks." Dottie gave him a stubborn look. "I'll get caught eventually, but until then, I'm gonna save as many as I can. You make sure Captain Hack checks in on my grandkids, okay?"

Beck smiled sadly. "It's General Hack now, and you bet your ass we'll watch out for your family. They heading to Charybdis Station?"

She nodded. "I'm sending everyone I can to the Anchor's Rest system or Tammol." Her comm chimed, and she looked down at it. "Gotta move on."

"Dottie?"

She looked up. "Yeah?"

"Thank you. For everything you've done for us, and everything you're doing for your planet. We're gonna do our best to make this better."

Her eyes softened, and she reached up to pat his cheek. "I know you will. Even when you all were mercenaries, you were honorable. I wish Vextonar was a better place."

"Maybe one day it will be."

Dottie left, and Beck checked on Lerais. He was still fueling up the Blue Sparrow, so Beck went in to talk to Dru.

"Hey, Beck," Fire said as he ran past. Two guinea pigs chased after the Element, rolling quickly in their balls.

Beck shook his head and grinned. He found Dru in the training room with Morgan and Alois. They watched Sebastian and Death train Remy and a young woman.

Sebastian's apprentice was an interesting man. He had been captured by the Concords on Union Station, then tortured. By the time they had managed to rescue him, it had been too late. The man had died.

Beck still didn't really understand how he'd been

resurrected, but he had. It had changed the way he looked, but as far as they could tell, he was the same man he had been before. His cat, Potato, still adored him in any case.

The cat watched Sebastian from beside Dru, eyes following every move Remy made.

"How's it going?" Beck nudged Dru with his shoulder, and she jumped.

"We're not dead yet," she said and shrugged. Monty scrambled from her shoulder to her head, unhappy with the movement.

"Is Remy making progress?"

Alois moved closer. "Death says he catches on even better than Sebastian did. I wonder if it's because he died. He says he doesn't remember anything about it, but that has to have an effect, right?"

Beck shrugged. "I know metal, circuits, and wires. Don't ask me. Who's the woman?"

"Jalyn. She's a soldier from Xav's ship and decided she wanted to train with Sebastian." Dru grinned. "You should have seen Xav's face. He was shocked as hell. Apparently, she's friends with Remy and is already close to *awakening,* or whatever the fuck they called it."

Morgan looked thoughtful. "As much as I hate the Queen and the asshole Elements, it makes me happy to see something of the Crells survive. Their species may be gone now, but Crellic shamanism and their history still goes on."

Beck nodded. "Yeah. That's not too bad, is it?"

Lerais came in and wrapped Dru in his arms. "Captain Sweet Mama, we're fueled and ready to go."

"I better get back to my own ship." Beck waved goodbye and went back to the Blue Solace, checking on the other ships on his way.

"Dad," Icarus said. He waited with Beol, Sax, and Meggie at the ramp. "We were worried. Why didn't you come back to the ship right away?"

Dr. Bloop sat at Beol's feet and gave Beck a stern look. He wore his Blue Solace vest and goggles today.

"This is not the place to go wandering, Beck." Meggie glared at him with her hands on her hips.

"I'm sorry," he said, wincing. "I wanted to check on the others. We're leaving now, so don't worry too much."

"I'll let Selene know you're alive," Sax said, turning away from him. "She was worried."

Beck smiled fondly. "*She* was worried?"

Sax looked over her shoulder. "Maybe it was me."

Icarus watched her walk away, and Beck sighed. "Rus, are you attracted to Sax?"

Meggie snorted. "You're only now asking? The man is crazy about her."

Icarus looked at them in horror. "Am I obvious? I know she can do so much better than me."

Beck huffed. "No one is better than you."

"She would be lucky to have you," Beol added.

Meggie patted Icarus's arm. "Pay a little more attention, big guy, and you'll notice how she watches you too."

Beck bit his lip. "Son, do we need to have *the talk*? I built you both, so I know what parts you've got."

Meggie leaned against Beol, laughing hard. "Oh,

please, Beck. Please give him *the talk*. Do you have any hand puppets?"

Beck gave her a disgruntled look. "It's perfectly natural to have questions, Meggie. Icarus? Do you have any questions?"

Icarus groaned and pressed his hands to his cheeks. "If I could blush, I would be blushing. No, Dad. I don't have questions. Our programming was thorough in explaining our biology."

"You sound like a bot," Meggie said. She deepened her voice. "Our programming was thorough, boop, boop, beep, beep."

Beck snickered.

Icarus gave them all a disgusted look. "Fuck you all. I'm going to make a cake."

He left, and Dr. Bloop followed him, nose in the air. "Woof."

Beck and Beol turned their attention to Meggie.

She arched a brow, smirking. "What?"

Beck crossed his arms. "What about you? Do you have your eye on anyone?"

She looked sad for a moment. "We don't have souls, do we? I really like someone, but what if his life-mate shows up one day?"

"Why do you think you don't have a soul?" Beol frowned. "I know you were created, but you're sentient. You're a person. I would think that means you have a soul."

Meggie shrugged. "I'm afraid to ask Death. If he confirms we don't, I'll know I can never have Dannol."

"Dannol!" Beck grinned. "Oh, Meggie. He's a really good guy."

She smiled. "We talk a lot. He has to stay on the bridge most of the time, and he doesn't sleep much. I even like his rooster, Hector." Her smile disappeared, and she gave them a self-deprecating look. "He's a Havenite, Beck. He would be able to tell if we were lifemates, and he hasn't said anything."

Beck felt the ship take off. "I need to go check on something."

He started toward his room, Meggie and Beol's eyes following him.

"You had better not ask Death about souls, Beck," Meggie ordered.

"I won't," he said. "Promise."

Once he reached the engineering bay, he pulled up his comm and called Sebastian.

Sebastian's face popped up. "Hey, Beck. We're training right now. Is it important?"

"You said you saw Icarus and the girls' threads, right?"

Sebastian grinned. "Yeah. All three of them are beautiful. Icarus has a lot of you in him, and Sax reminds me of a mixture of Selene and Beol."

"What about Meggie?"

"Meggie is… Meggie. She's quirky and sweet, but beyond intelligent. I know you don't want to hear this, but she's smarter than your Icarus and Sax both."

Beck grinned proudly. "She is really smart." His grin faded, and he sighed. "Do you think they have souls?"

Death's face appeared in Sebastian's place. The man

must have grabbed Sebastian's wrist and pulled it toward him.

"They do have souls, Beck. I'm a little put out you haven't asked me about it."

Beck shrugged. "Never thought of it until now. Sorry, Dr. Morrick."

"All three of your Bracken have beautiful souls," Death said. "As Dr. Morrick, quantifying souls is impossible, and I hate even thinking of trying to prove their existence, but as Death, it's simple. I see their souls."

Beck hummed happily. "Thank you. I have a pilot to talk to."

"No, you don't."

Beol's voice came from behind him, and Beck jumped, yelping, as he turned around. He ended the call without saying goodbye.

"I didn't ask Death anything," Beck said hurriedly. "He just volunteered information. I was talking to Sebastian."

Beol held a dagger in his right hand and flipped it over and over again. "I went straight to the source. I had a little chat with Dannol. Meggie is young, and I don't want him taking advantage of her."

"Oh," Beck said, hugging his tail to him. "I get all shivery when you go badass assassin on people. What did he say?"

Beol scowled and stopped flipping his dagger. "He'll talk to her later. It's not our business apparently."

Beck gasped in outrage. "He didn't tell you?"

"No. I even showed him my favorite weapons and threatened to eat his chicken."

"Dannol refused to tell you? Our sweet, hug-addicted Dannol?"

"I know, right?" Beol looked disgusted. "I think I'm losing my edge. It's probably all the smiling I do now."

"Hmm. Do you want to practice interrogating someone? Maybe you will find a Grell mechanic stowed away on your ship, and you need to punish him?"

Beol looked at him in consideration as he started flipping his dagger again. "What are you doing on my ship?"

14

THE CRELLIC SYSTEM - TWO WEEKS LATER

*B*eol watched Selene and Sax spar in the training center. He felt queasy watching them move around, and his stomach felt *heavy*. That didn't even make sense, and he was the one feeling it.

Tinker sat on his shoulder. She curled against his neck and pressed her cool hands against his jaw. She hummed softly, doing her best to soothe him.

"Eat a cracker." Leti sat beside him and handed him a pack of crackers.

Princess settled his large head on Leti's lap, watching Beol with narrowed eyes.

Beol growled. "I don't want food."

"It'll make you feel better. Eat it."

"I don't like you."

Leti grinned. "Yes, you do. Who else, besides Beck, will put up with your grumpy ass?"

It's true, Beol thought. He'd never been the sweetest person in the galaxy, but now he was constantly irritable.

Yesterday, Princess Buttercup had hissed at him as they passed each other in the hallway, and Beol had actually hissed back. He didn't know who he shocked more – himself or Princess.

Leti's Fyrling, Jenks, flew in lazy circles above Leti's head. She looked a bit like Tinker, but she was a mix of chrome and purple. Her long, white dreadlocks swished as she flew.

Occasionally, she would fly off to inspect something, usually by running into it, but she always returned to her person. She might not be the smartest Fyrling around, but at least she was sweet and loyal.

Beol nibbled on a cracker. "You're annoyingly perky all the time, your sweaters are ugly, and your dragon scares people."

"It'll be alright, Beol. Hormones can be a pain in the butthole." Leti pulled Beol's head down to rest on his shoulder, and Princess rumbled unhappily. "It's funny; when I was pregnant, I snapped at Will and Sebastian the most and tried to be nice to everyone else. You're the opposite. You're sweet as can be to Beck and Icarus, but Mr. Grumpy to the rest of us."

"I love Beck and Icarus. I barely tolerate the rest of you."

"Really? Is that why you gave your newest vibro-blade to Selene and sewed that button back on my favorite llama sweater?"

"How did you know that was me?"

"Draif and Ava are the only ones I know who can sew that well. Plus, I saw you doing it. You snuck into the bathroom in the cargo bay."

"Stop stalking me. You're everywhere I go."

"I can't help it. It's a little boring without the kids, and Will occasionally has to work. Do you want me to tell you what I saw Dannol and Meggie doing?"

"Gods, no. She's like a daughter to me. I prefer to think of her as innocent and virginal for the rest of my life."

Leti laughed, then whispered in Beol's ear. "He called her mate."

Beol couldn't stop his grin. "I still don't like you."

"No, you love me. I'm your best friend."

"You stole Wolfe from me."

Leti snorted. "I'm Wolfe's friend. You're his brother. Trust me, Wolfe loves you more than anything."

"Then why won't he live with the guild?"

Leti stroked his hair, and Beol wondered why he was still leaning on the annoying man.

"I think he wanted to feel normal for a bit. He never got to be anything other than an assassin, right?"

"He doesn't want to be part of the guild?"

"Come on, Beol. How much of a guild do you really have anymore? You and Half-Moon are part of Charybdis Station now."

"The Lord Admiral wants to make us a special ops division. He wants to make me the Purple General. I hate fucking purple. Why does it have to be a color?"

Leti chuckled. "He'd probably negotiate the name."

"Yeah. Probably."

"Do you want to do it? Become an official part of Charybdis Station?"

"I presented it to the guild before we left. I'm giving

them time to think about it, then Bendix will call a vote."

"I think Wolfe would like that, being part of something bigger than a guild."

"Yeah."

Hack's voice came through the ship's comm. He sounded upset. "Everyone, please come to the conference room."

Leti gave Beol a worried look. "This can't be good."

Leti and Beol followed Selene and Sax to the conference room. Beck stood with Hack. Both men looked furious. Beol slipped under Beck's arm, pressing into his mate's side. Anger wasn't a natural state of being for Beck, and Beol didn't like it.

"Everyone here?" Hack looked around. "Dru and the other captains are telling the rest of the ships now. Draif sent us a video from early this morning on Vextonar."

He pushed his tablet, and the video appeared on the large vid-screen at the front of the room.

A young, nervous-looking human reporter stood in front of the Capital Building on Vextonar.

"This is Jen Rally, standing in for Larry Sutton. I'm live at the Capital Building of the Prime on Vextonar, in the Silverlight System. Recently, the Vextonian government requested media coverage for an important announcement. Here they come now."

A middle-aged human woman stepped up to the podium situated at the top of the stairs. The gathered reporters started yelling out questions, but she just smiled. Beol noticed every reporter he could see looked human.

She held up a hand for silence. *"Thank you for joining us today. I will attempt to keep this brief. Vextonar is one of the best, if not the best, planet in the galaxy. We pride ourselves on our purity, intelligence, and wealth. As the President of Vextonar, I have worked with our Congress of Prime to bring our planet to the next stage of greatness. Today, Vextonar is pleased to announce we are joining the renowned coalition, Humans First."*

The crowd of reporters erupted with questions. The woman held her hands up again.

"Please, no questions. The Prime of Vextonar recognize greatness can only be achieved when we 'cut the fat away.' Last night, all citizens that were not at least eighty percent human were arrested. We don't want our planet to be home to lesser species.

"Our dear friends in Humans First suggested we rid the galaxy of these mutts, but we've chosen to show mercy. We have sold these lesser species and hybrids, so they can serve a greater purpose. If you wish to purchase one, please contact the Vextonian embassy on your planet."

Beol exchanged horrified looks with the others in the room. "Is this for real?"

"Dottie was right," Beck whispered, laying his chin on top of Beol's head.

"During the gathering last night, we made some horrible discoveries. Some humans—pure humans—were committing treasonous acts against our species by aiding the filth that has plagued our planet."

Behind her, seven people were led out of the

building. They each had their hands tied behind their backs.

The young reporter gasped and covered her mouth. *"There's Larry. Oh gods, there's Larry."*

Leti cried out. "Is that Dottie?"

"Yeah," Beck said, voice cracking.

"For their crimes, they will be publicly executed. We will not stand for treason against our great planet."

Dottie pushed forward, shouting, *"This isn't about Vextonar. It's not about humans. It's about greed and cruelty. You've sold over sixty percent of your population into slavery. That's treason, you stupid bitch. If you think all of humanity will let you get away with this, you underestimate us."*

The woman nodded to the guards. *"Kill them."*

Each guard pulled a phaser and shot a prisoner in the back of the head. Dottie's body crumpled to the ground.

The reporter turned to look into the camera, tears streaming down her face. She was pale and looked frightened. *"Larry's dead. I can't believe this. That was Dottie too. She was my friend. I don't... I don't know what to say."*

The vid-screen went black and the room was completely silent. Beol hugged Beck tightly, knowing how much his mate had admired Dottie.

Hack finally broke the silence. "HF will pay for this. Draif and Ava, as unlikely as it may seem, will see them ruined."

Leti leaned into his mate, sobbing.

"They have their first base of operations," Selene

said. "They'll likely control Union Station too. Those are the only two settled planets in the Silverlight System."

"Draif said they've also taken Rueal in the Sugarworm System," Hack said.

"I need to check on Pela's parents," Rune said, shaking himself out of the stupor they all were feeling.

"Morgan and Wyatt already did," Hack said. "Pela's family moved to Tammol a few weeks ago. Rueal was becoming uncomfortable for any non-human or hybrid."

"How are people reacting to this?" Beol stroked his mate's back.

"Not well," Hack answered. "HF endorsed the destruction of planets, but this is the first time they've visibly taken part in the killing. Humans across the galaxy are protesting their actions, and Draif said the stock in the four leaders' corporations just plummeted. For some reason, their customers don't want to be associated with them."

"They didn't have to use the Queen this time, did they?" Dannol sighed, and Meggie wrapped her arms around him.

"What about Dottie's family?" Beol remembered Beck mentioning she had sent her family to Charybdis Station.

"They arrived on Charybdis a few days ago," Hack said, rubbing his hand over his face. "They're good folks, but they're not handling this well. A lot of our people knew and loved Dottie."

"She ran the spaceport," Selene said. "Many knew and admired her."

"She could have left and been safe," Beck said. "She stayed behind to help as many as she could. She knew this would probably happen."

"She was a brave woman," Leti said, fighting back a sob. "She risked a lot to help me and Draif get off planet and practically handed me to Will. President Wineon will regret what she did today. We'll make sure of it."

Beol walked with Beck back to their room. Beck hadn't said much, but Beol knew his mate was hurting. Tinker flew to Beck's shoulder and hugged his face, cooing softly. Beol sighed. She really didn't understand boundaries.

"I'm sorry, Beck."

"I wish I had just grabbed her and made her come with us."

"How many do you think she saved in two weeks?"

Tinker flew to her house, and Beck pulled him into his arms. "Don't make me say it."

Beol settled his head against Beck's chest. "The Queen and her Elements have killed billions of people, likely under direction of HF. This though. This shocks me. They're stepping into the light as the monsters they are. Why risk their businesses?"

Beck sighed. "I'll leave that for Draif and Ava to figure out. I just want the fuckers dead."

15

CRELLIC SYSTEM, EN ROUTE TO PLANET
GENARG - ONE WEEK LATER

Beck turned his tablet off and rubbed his eyes. Beol slept peacefully beside him while Bloop curled up on Beck's other side. Tinker hummed softly from her house.

Leti had given Beck a few of the Crellic books to read when he complained he couldn't fall asleep a few days ago, but reading about the Queen and her Elements didn't exactly relax him.

He leaned down and kissed Beol's head, then slid out of bed.

"Going to visit Icarus?" Beol didn't even open his eyes.

"I thought you were asleep."

"Sparky, I'm a trained assassin."

"Yet, Leti keeps sneaking in to visit you." Beck grinned. Leti was about as sneaky as Bloop, which was not at all.

Beol opened one eye. "I don't like him."

"Sure, you don't," Beck said, slowly, backing out of

the room. "Big, badass assassin loves Leti the llama king."

Beol groaned and rolled over to bury his face in his pillow.

Beck laughed as the door shut behind him. His grumpy kitty was so cute. He made his way to the commons.

Icarus tended the plants hanging in the room. His fern, Fawn, had a special place set up in the corner.

"Hey, Dad. Did you need something to eat? How about a cup of cocoa?"

Beck smiled softly. "I'm fine, Rus. I just can't sleep."

"We're approaching Genarg now." Icarus grabbed his hand and pulled him over to the window.

A large green and blue planet dominated the view. Clouds swirled in Genarg's atmosphere, and two small moons slowly orbited the planet.

"It looks a lot like the humans' home world did, doesn't it?" Icarus squeezed his hand. "Are you nervous, Dad?"

"Yeah," he admitted. "We've been really lucky so far, but this is the most unprepared we've been going into a mission. Then, there's the fact I'm going to be sitting on the shuttle while my pregnant mate heads off to try to kill a monster."

"Beol *is* the better fighter," Icarus said.

"I have my bots."

"Now, so does almost everyone else."

Beck had spent the trip training the crews of their five ships on using the neuro-control implant. So far, each person had managed to successfully control at least one bot. Selene had the most at three bots.

"It doesn't mean I wouldn't be a help."

"They need an extraction team, Dad. Someone has to lead it."

Beck sighed. "Stop making sense, Rus."

The plan was for the small fleet to split into two teams and fly down to the planet on shuttles. The scouts had located both Earth and the Queen. They were on opposite sides of the only occupied town on the planet.

Earth had built his Queen a huge temple using prisoners the Concords were continuously dropping off on Genarg. A small town had recently sprung up around it. The soldiers and mercenaries had to live somewhere, after all.

One team would head to the center of the city, where the Queen dwelled, and the other team would head to the edge of the town where Earth stayed in the prisoner camp.

A light crew would remain on both shuttles in case the teams needed to be extracted. Beck's shuttle would hold him, Leti and his guards, Rune, Meggie, Sax, and Icarus.

If the two teams failed, the shuttles would return to the ships, and they'd retreat as fast as they could.

It was a shit plan, and they all knew it. "What choice do we have?" Beck asked quietly.

Beck sat with Icarus for a few hours, talking about everything and nothing. Slowly, the rest of the ship woke up as they moved closer to the planet.

Hack stared out the window as he ate his breakfast. "That's twenty-eight ships we've passed so far, and we aren't even to the planet yet. Beol's scouts weren't kidding when they said the place was swarming with HF's people."

"I've seen the ships of six different mercenary groups," Selene said. "I don't recognize the others."

"They're ships from the HF leaders' personal armies," Leti said. "I recognize fucking Cortez's crest."

"Why do you hate him so much?" Selene tilted her head. "It's more than the fact he leads HF."

"His son hurt Draif." Leti's eyes were furious.

Beol's arms wrapped around Beck, and he felt his mate press his face against his back. Beck threaded his fingers through Beol's.

"They'll both die, Leti," Beol said. "It's on our to-do list."

Dannol's voice came over the ship's comm. "We're approaching the planetary defenses."

Beol's comm chimed, and Beck turned around in his arms.

They all watched as Noe's face appeared above Beol's wrist. "Hey, boss-man. Our scouts just boarded Moyra's damn ship."

"It's called the Blue Moyra. Say it!" Moyra's voice came over the line, and Noe rolled his eyes.

"Anyway, they found a blind spot in Genarg's planetary defenses. They've been slipping through for months now. I'll send you the coordinates."

"I'm impressed," Selene said. "The defense looks

impenetrable, but your scouts have entered several times now."

"One of my scouts, Alber, said the defense system was exactly like the one set up around Tammol, so he was familiar with it," Beol said. "He was one of mine that helped Jody take the planet."

An hour later, they all piled into the conference room. The vid-screen showed the conference rooms of the four other ships.

"Alright," Hack said. "It's time to finish this. I lead team one against the Queen with Death and Sebastian. Dru leads team two against Earth with Fire and Remy."

"As a brief reminder," Death said. "The Queen is far more powerful than she looks. She controls all Elements with an unimaginable expertise. Brute force simply won't work. Stealth and the unexpected are our only true allies."

"Earth is complicated," Fire added. "The planet he's on is his main source of power, in this case, Genarg. He controls everything on this planet, from tectonic plates beneath the surface to the trees and soil above. He could destroy Genarg, and all of us with it, in a heartbeat."

Beck hugged Beol tightly. It was so strange to see Fire serious and in charge. It was easy to forget that the Element was ancient when he was chasing guinea pigs around, or raiding their fridge. He had thrown a fit when it was decided that he wouldn't be going with Sebastian. Now, he stood beside Dru, face grim.

"We've prepared as much as we can," Hack said. "I know we're going into this half-cocked, but I know that if anyone can do this, it's us. We must protect the galaxy and our home from the Queen."

Beck kissed Beol gently as the crew started filing out of the room. "You'll be careful, right?"

"Of course," Beol said. "I may bitch about the babies, but I love them, and I love you. I'll do my damnedest to come out of this alive."

Beck checked the ship over one more time, Beol glued to his side, then walked Dr. Bloop to the bridge. Tinker perched on the dog's head and chittered worriedly. All the pets would stay on board with Dannol and Nettle, well except Princess, but he was a Charybdis soldier now.

"Be a good boy, Dr. Bloop," Beol said, rubbing the dog's ears. "Your dog dad is here, and he'll be worried about his people too. Keep each other company, okay? Keep an eye on Tinker."

Hack kissed the top of Gravy's head. "They'll take care of one another. Right boy?"

Gravy licked Hack's face, then trotted over to sit next to Bloop.

"Come on, assassin," Hack said, slapping Beol's back. "Let's get this over with so I can love on my mate."

Leti sniffled and pressed against Hack's side. "If you don't come back, we'll find you and drag your ass back, Will."

Princess Buttercup met them at the shuttle.

"He wants to go with us," Leti said, voice breaking. "He can't sneak with you guys, but he can stay on the ship with me."

Hack looked relieved. "I'd actually really like that. Thanks, Princess."

The dragon eyed him.

"Yeah, yeah. I love you too." Hack rolled his eyes.

Beck went to the pilot's seat and started the shuttle up. He looked back and counted heads, then headed to Xav's ship to pick up his crew, then on to Moyra's ship to get part of the Half-Moon folks. Dru would have Haroon's crew and the rest of Half-Moon.

"Guild Master." Clara nodded as she boarded with Wolfe, Noe, and a few others. "There's a path from the closest jungle that leads straight to the heart of the temple."

"That's not very sensible," Selene said.

Clara shrugged. "I know what you mean. The mercs and the rest stay away from the temple because the Queen and her guards are creepy as hell. There were too many of them to take on with just the five of us scouts or we would have given it a try."

"She would have killed you all," Death said.

"So, you say," Clara said, making a face. "She doesn't do anything but pace around."

"We can't trust appearances." Death shook his head. "She's a very social person, so that's very unusual, but she's also devious."

Beck followed the coordinates and flew into the blind spot. He landed outside of the town, in a clearing a little way into the jungle, and lowered the back ramp.

He held Beol's hand as they unloaded. His mate's face was stoic, and Beck knew he was mentally preparing himself for the fight.

Death swallowed hard, sadness filling his eyes. "It's strange being back here. The jungle looks and smells like it always has. Like home. I wish Wyatt had come on the shuttle so I could show him this." He shook his head. "What am I saying? He's safer on the ship."

Hack pulled Leti into his arms, and everyone looked away, trying to give them a moment.

"What the fuck are those?" Clara pointed at the bots swirling in the air.

"Beck's bots," Noe said, shrugging. "You miss things when you volunteer to scout out a distant planet, Clara."

Beck looked at Beol. Noe actually sounded angry. Did he and Clara have a thing?

Beol shrugged.

Clara arched a brow. "They'll stand out a bit, don't you think?"

Almost as one, each person focused, and the bots disappeared from vision.

"Damn," she said. "They're shielded?"

"Yeah. They also have sensors that prevent them from running into one another," Beck said, trying to smile.

"I wish I had a sensor that did that," Morgan said. "There's benefits to invisibility, but there are also some downsides."

"That's amazing," Clara said, smiling. "I want one."

"We make it through this, I'll get you one."

Beol hugged him. "Don't worry so much, Sparky. We'll come back."

"You had better. I don't know how I'll make it if you don't. Plus, you've got our sons baking in there."

"You're pregnant?" Clara looked flabbergasted. "Why didn't anyone pass that gossip on?"

Hack patted him on the shoulder. "You'll watch out for Leti? I'll keep an eye on Beol."

Beck nodded. He'd guard Leti with his life.

Beck wished he could keep Beol in his arms, but he had to let him go. Beol kissed his cheek, hugged Icarus and the girls, then went to stand with Noe and Wolfe, who was currently being hugged/mauled by Leti.

"I'll make sure he comes back, Beck." Selene hugged him, settling her head on his chest.

"Make sure you come back too," he said, voice cracking. "This isn't a normal mission."

"No. It's not." She pushed away and went with the others.

Together, they activated their shields and disappeared.

Beck turned around. "Everyone back on the ship. We need to stay ready in case they need us."

They loaded back up, and Beck sat in the pilot's seat, praying to every god he could think of.

———

Beck checked the time. It felt like it had been hours, but only fifteen minutes had passed. He scanned the clearing. Nothing but a few animals around.

Leti leaned against the back of his seat, Princess in

his arms. The dragon was his traveling size, and Beck hoped he didn't have to change that.

Leti hugged his dragon tightly, lip trembling. "I know I'm supposed to be strong, and I know Will is one of the best, but I'm so scared, Beck. This plan just plain sucks."

"We have to believe in them," Beck said.

Princess lifted his head and hissed. The shuttle rocked, and the windows were quickly covered by thick branch-like vines.

"What the fuck is that?" Silas jumped up with the rest, and they looked around the shuttle as it creaked.

Beck looked up from the scan. "The scan doesn't show anything, and our comm is out. Maia, take the pilot's seat."

The young woman hurried over.

Beck walked through the shuttle, trying to look out each of the windows. Vines covered everything.

He focused, and his six bots flew from the upper storage space, circling his head. "Sax and Icarus stay with Leti. Silas, come with me. Everyone keep your injectors handy."

Beck pushed the button and opened the hatch door. He didn't expect it or the ramp to work, but the door slid open, clear of vines. What the hell was going on?

He stepped outside and saw her. The young woman looked feral. She was Silet, with long, tangled, white hair. Like every other member of her species, her pink skin sparkled like it was covered in glitter, but she was covered in mud and dirt. Cleaned up, she would be beautiful. As she was, she looked like she lived in the jungle.

Her eyes caught his attention. Most Silet had very human-looking eyes, but hers were completely black – sclera and iris, the whole thing.

"Earth?"

She nodded. "That's what they call me this cycle."

Beck raised his phaser, and Silas did the same. "I'm guessing you want something, seeing as how we aren't dead yet."

She looked uncertain. "I... I don't know. You're from Charybdis Station. Correct?"

"We are," Leti said, peeking around him.

Beck turned and glared at Icarus and Sax. The two androids had their weapons drawn.

Sax blinked. "We stayed with Leti."

"You're Leti Hackett," Earth said. "My Queen despises you."

Leti frowned. "Why me?"

"She had plans, but you figured things out and made us public knowledge."

"Plans?" Leti looked curious.

"She intended to stay in the background and use the Concords and Humans First to destroy the galaxy, but you made sure everyone knew of us and our history."

Earth's eyes kept slipping to Sax and Icarus, though she tried to keep her attention on Leti. Finally, she seemed to give up on it.

"What *are* you two? You're living, but not alive. I've never seen anything like you."

"They're my children," Beck said, moving in front of

them. "Don't you even think of hurting them."

"Children?"

"My name is Beck. I made them."

Earth's eyes widened. "You *made* them."

"What do you want, Earth?" Leti frowned at the woman. "This isn't exactly how we pictured this confrontation going."

"No," she said softly. "I don't imagine you would have."

"I know pieces of your history, your story," Leti said. "I know you love the Queen and are her most loyal Element."

Beck whined at the pain in her eyes. He had never seen agony like that.

Her eyes met his. "Come with me, Beck. Bring your children and come with me. I need to show you something."

"He goes, we all go," Leti said, voice firm.

"No," Beck said. "You need to stay with the shuttle in case… just in case."

"The shuttle isn't going anywhere," Maia said from the door. "There are flowers growing in the engine."

"Bring your friends, creator, but come. I need to show you something."

"Alright," Beck said. "We'll come with you."

If they were with Earth, that meant that Dru's team wasn't. They would try to contact everyone and notice Beck's shuttle was out of commission. Hopefully.

Everyone filed out of the shuttle and followed the woman into the jungle.

eol walked down the path toward the temple, eyes scanning the area. Clara was right. No one was even close to them. The temple should have been covered with protection for the Queen.

"Entering the temple now." Hack's voice echoed in his earpiece.

The temple was a large, pyramid-shaped building with an ornate staircase starting at the base. It was surrounded by lush, beautifully kept gardens and paths.

"The Queen's sanctum is at the very top," Clara said. "The main stairs lead straight to it."

"Everyone stay to the right on the stairs," Hack said.

The group easily climbed the stairs, meeting no one on the way.

"This isn't right," Death said. "Something is wrong."

The stairs led to a large, opulent, and airy room. Several men and women stood to attention along the walls, eyes straight ahead.

The Queen paced back and forth in front of a delicate, golden throne. She wore a Silet body, Dr. Linda Belcort to be exact. She was dressed in a simple white dress with a golden belt.

Beol stood still, looking around the room. No one noticed them. The Queen continued her pacing, unaware of their presence. Death was right. Something wasn't right.

Fire's voice came through the earpiece, frantic. "Earth isn't here. It was just a golem."

Golem?

Someone – it could have been anyone really – stabbed the queen with the injector.

She stopped pacing and stood still. Beol finally noticed her eyes. They were blank and completely empty.

Death deactivated his shield. "That's not her. It's just a golem. The guards are soulless husks, likely golems as well."

Beol walked to the nearest one and sliced the man in two with his blade. It crumbled to dust.

Someone did the same to the Queen, and her body crumbled into little bits.

"Fuck," Hack said. "Retreat back to the ships. We'll regroup and figure shit out."

"I'm so sorry," Clara said, voice shaking. "We didn't get close to her, so we didn't know. Fuck. I'm so sorry."

"You did exactly what you were supposed to," Beol said. "Let's get out of here."

They hurried back to the shuttle and deactivated

their shields. Beol froze, heart stopping at the sight of the shuttle covered in vines. "Beck."

"Leti," Hack called out, running toward the shuttle. He disappeared inside for only a second before coming back out.

"They aren't there."

"Dead?" Beol didn't recognize his voice. It was so empty.

"No," Hack said, clapping him on the back. "No signs of a fight. No blood. No dead bodies."

"I called Dru. Her shuttle is on the way," Noe said.

"They went this way," Selene said. She stood at the edge of the jungle. "I count nine sets of footprints."

"Nine? There were only eight of them," Clara said. "Well, if you don't count Princess Buttercup."

A shuttle landed, and Dru and the others poured out. "What happened?"

Fire flew to Sebastian's side, hugging him tightly.

"Let's find out," Hack said grimly.

They followed Selene as she tracked the footprints.

It seemed like ages, but may have only been about half an hour, before they found them.

Beol recognized Earth. He wore Melinda Belcort's body and stood with Beck and Meggie, looking down into some kind of pit. Beol moved quickly to his mate's side, eyes searching out Icarus and Sax.

Leti cried out and ran to Hack when he saw him, but Earth didn't look up.

"The Queen?" Leti looked from face to face, counting heads.

"Golem," Death answered. His eyes were glued to

Earth. "Earth, what are you doing? Where is the Queen?"

Earth looked over his shoulder. "I don't know. She's been with her humans for months now. She ordered the golem made as a distraction."

"She knew about the scouts?" Hack arched a brow. "Why not kill them?"

Earth shook his head. "She didn't know about the scouts. My planet is crawling with humans, and she wanted to keep them all on their toes. Your scouts came after she left."

"Why not kill us if you knew about us?" Clara moved closer to the pit.

Earth shrugged. "Why bother?"

"Beol?" Beck's voice was strained. "Can you come here?"

"I'm already here." Beol tried not to smile when Beck jumped.

His mate wrapped his arms around him and picked him up in a huge hug. Beol's feet dangled off the ground, but he couldn't make himself care.

"I'm glad you're alive."

"Me too."

Beck turned him toward the pit. "Look down there."

Beol peered into the pit, unimpressed. Inside were sixteen piles of dirt. "Dirt?"

"Meggie scanned them," Beck whispered.

Meggie blinked at Beol, clearly still in shock. "Uh, yeah."

A small screen opened in her palm, and she showed Beol the results.

Beol's mouth fell open. "What?"

"Earth, what have you done?" Death surveyed the piles, looking as shocked as Beol felt.

Beol pushed at Beck's shoulders, finally getting his mate to put him down. He turned to the Element, watching him closely. He recognized the defeat in Earth's eyes.

He had felt that same thing when his mom killed Lolita. When he had known she would never be the woman he thought she was.

Beol tilted his head. "Where's your loyalty, Earth?"

Earth looked at Beol, then at the pit. "The Belcorts woke the Queen first. Each cycle starts the same. Our Queen is awakened by our people. They beg her to help them against some enemy, and she raises her Elements. Then she manipulates her people until they destroy themselves."

"What changed?" Beol asked. "What's different this time?"

"The Belcorts' pilot was human. When he realized what the Belcorts were going to do, he called a friend of his and the Concords arrived. Three men and one woman came with them. I don't know how he convinced them to come."

"The leaders of Humans First?" Leti tugged Hack closer to the pit and peered inside.

"Yes," Earth said. "Before any of us were raised, they spoke to my Queen. *They* made the request, and she raised us."

"Okay, so I'm still not seeing what was different?"

Dru walked over and looked in the pit. Monty stared down from her head. "Dirt? Woohoo."

"Your people weren't the ones to raise her," Beck said quietly. "Because they're all gone, extinct."

Earth's face twisted in agony. "Our people are dead. There is not one living Crell in all the galaxy, and it is our fault. We drove them to this. When I awoke this cycle, our system lay dormant and empty, and *she* was only concerned with finding someone to manipulate. Someone to bleed for her."

"Earth," Fire said. He tugged Sebastian behind him as he went to Earth to hug him. "I didn't even think of that."

Earth sank against Fire. "My Queen is gone. My love, my mate, is truly gone. All I've done for her, all the pain I caused, was for nothing. She will never come back. I see it now."

They were quiet as the Element sobbed.

"In her original lifetime, the Queen wanted peace," Leti said softly. "She wanted to protect her people."

Earth turned his face, keeping his head on Fire's shoulder. "She was magnificent, so brave and kind. We bonded to her, and she wielded our power for the good of her people."

"The ritual to bring her back corrupted her soul," Sebastian said.

"Each time they brought her back, I hoped that something would change," Earth said. "I hoped she would be herself again."

"You served her loyally all those cycles," Death said. "You just hoped she would change?"

"I hoped the shamans would be able to cleanse her soul." Earth looked at Sebastian. "Is there any way?"

Sebastian hesitated, then shared a look with Death. "I think, maybe, there is."

"It would mean killing her," Death said.

"Tell me how," Earth demanded, pushing away from Fire. "Tell me how to save her soul."

"We would need to kill her," Sebastian repeated. "Then, Death would need to freeze her soul, and I would need to do the cleansing ritual. Tell said it might work, but nothing is certain."

"Tell?" Earth smiled softly. "He's your spirit guide?"

"Yes," Sebastian said, smiling shyly. "If you peek into the spirit world, he's here now. He would love to talk to you when you're ready."

"The Queen hated the idea of you becoming a shaman. She enjoyed being the only one."

Fire stomped his foot. "Too bad. Sebastian's here now, and he's the best."

"Killing her is already going to be almost impossible," Hack said. "Do you really think we can do all this too?"

"We felt the others die," Earth said. "Why can't you kill her like you did them?"

Beol closed his eyes and thought for a moment as the people around them argued.

"Are you thinking of your father?" Beck asked.

Beol smiled, wondering why he was surprised Beck's thoughts were following his own. "Yes."

He turned to Earth. "She trusts you completely, doesn't she?"

Earth nodded.

"Our problem is getting close enough to her to inject her with the poison that killed the others. Water was killed with deception. Life was killed through the element of surprise. Air was killed by sheer luck and Sebastian's skill."

"She'll know you're coming," Earth said and gave Sebastian an apologetic look. "She is far more skilled than Sebastian."

"Plus, we've probably used up our quota of luck for the next fifty years," Dru said, sighing.

"She would never expect you to kill her," Beol said. "You're her former life-mate."

Earth opened his mouth, then closed it.

Hack's comm chimed, and they all jumped. "Fuck."

Dannol's face appeared, panicked. "General, Draif just called. Media coverage just showed the Queen destroying Port Broacia, then leaving with Cortez's personal fleet. She's not on Genarg."

"Yeah, we found that out," Hack said dryly.

"Ninetta is trailing them now. She was already in the Radiant System for some reason."

Beol smiled. "That reason would be a very lucrative contract on a murderous slaver."

Hack snorted. "Assassin's luck. Where are they headed?"

"She thinks they're coming to Charybdis Station. She managed to pick up some of the communication between ships."

"She'll be there in a month if that's where they're

going," Hack mused. "We've known they would target us at some point."

"If you want my help, we need to get her here," Earth said. "My power is connected to Genarg right now, and I can't leave."

Fire frowned. "Why not? Ships aren't so bad. I have guinea pigs I can show you. They're fun. What's it like having boobs?"

They all looked at Fire in horror, but Earth just shrugged. "I've never cared much for any of my bodies. I like being in my Elemental form. Breasts are alright, I guess."

Fire poked Earth's chest. "They're squishy."

"Fire," Sebastian hissed, knocking his hand away from Earth. "Boundaries."

"Earth," Beck said. "Ignore Fire. We need to explain this to them." He waved toward the pit.

Icarus and Sax moved to stand with them, and Beol leaned up to kiss his mate.

"Everyone will understand your secret," Beck said. "Trust me. They handled mine really well."

Leti scrunched his nose up. "You never did explain why Beck got so excited when you showed him those piles of dirt."

"My Queen wanted her planet revived and her temple built," Earth said. "They left me on Genarg while the rest of the Elements went with her to strategize with the Concords and Humans First."

"You revived this whole planet?" Leti gasped. "I saw pictures of it before. It was an empty rock with no life."

"It took most of a year and all my energy," Earth

said. "It's a good thing the planet was empty. It was a violent, chaotic rebirth. Genarg was revived, but there were no Crells. All that was left of them was bone and dust."

"How did you…?" Beck looked back in the pit.

"As I weaved through my planet, I gathered what was left of my people." Earth looked into the pit, and everyone gathered around, staring at the sixteen piles of dirt.

Earth waved his hand, and a bit of soil moved from one of the piles, sliding away so they could see the translucent encasement and the developing fetus within.

"Genarg and I will give life to my people again," Earth said.

Beck almost laughed at the looks on their faces. They had thought it wild when Becca, Gregor, and he had made sentient androids. At least he hadn't used a planet to grow babies.

"Am I really seeing what I'm seeing?" Dannol's voice was tinny through the comm, but Hack had given him a perfect view of the pit.

"Yep," Beck said, giving in and picking his mate up again. "Earth needs to stay here so she can keep growing the baby Crell. How are we gonna get the Queen here?"

"Beck," Death said, wincing. "Earth is a he. Just because his body is female, doesn't mean he is. He has never had a female host before."

"Actually, I don't really care," Earth said. "I'm an Element, a planet. I'm not a man or a woman. He, she, or they are all fine. Perhaps one day I will care though. One of my workers is nonbinary. They were kind enough to answer my questions. Having a body is always so complicated."

"It's okay, Earth. Bodies are kind of weird," Fire said. "I've never spent so much time in a body before, but I have a penis and sometimes it gets hard. Death says that's just fine, and that one day, my penis might get hard for someone special."

Death smacked his face. "Fire, I love you, but please, stop speaking."

Earth smiled softly. "Fire has always been Fire, but it's nice to see you unfrozen, Death. You thawed our last cycle, and now you are truly alive."

Death sighed. "It hurts sometimes, to live. My son makes it worth it."

"Death *really* likes living," Fire said. "I saw him fucking Val. He's Lorry's dad, and Lorry is Sai's life-mate."

"What?" Sebastian and everyone else stared at Death in surprise.

The man's face was red. "I think I would rather fight the Queen than be here right now."

Earth looked puzzled. "Who is Sai?"

"Oh, she's Sebastian's little sister."

Earth nodded at Death. "I'm glad you've found a lover. Sometimes I miss sex. A body is good for something after all. It can be an amazing thing."

Death groaned as everyone started laughing. "We have things to do, people. We need to call the station and figure out a plan."

"Come with me, Fire," Earth said. "I'll show you my

favorite tree, and we can gossip where Death won't hear us."

"Good idea. He's so weird sometimes. I like you like this, Earth. You're like you were before we died the first time."

The two walked into the jungle, and Dru looked worried. "Um, we just let Fire leave with Earth. Shouldn't we be worried? What if this is a ploy to separate us?"

Beck looked into the pit. "She left us with the baby pods. She wouldn't have done that if she didn't trust us."

"Okay," Hack said, letting out a deep breath. "This didn't go quite the way we thought it would, but damn it, we're still alive, so that's something. Dru, will you take a few people back and get the shuttle? I guess the other shuttle is done for."

"It needs some work, but it's out of commission right now," Maia said.

"Lerais, Morgan, Quinn come with me." Dru headed back the way they had come.

"If the Queen reaches Charybdis Station, she'll destroy it," Death said.

"We need her here," Hack said, sighing. "My kids are on that station, damn it. It's our home."

"Earth said the Queen manipulates people to bring about their own destruction," Leti said. "We assumed HF was pulling her strings, but she's using them. That explains why they've been doing so many stupid things. Draif said the four leaders have lost a lot of money."

"Yeah," Sebastian agreed. "For appearances sake

though, HF controls her, and we need her here, but HF doesn't care about Genarg. It's too far away from anything important, and she wouldn't let them farm it for resources."

Beol thought about the broadcast from Vextonar. "What if we take Genarg? What if we make it public knowledge that we're here and it's ours? Splash it all over the media?"

"That would get her attention," Death said, eyes widening. "We would need to somehow explain Earth. The Queen can't know he's our ally, but she'll know he isn't dead."

"Earth said she liked to be part of the planet," Beck said. "Would it be plausible to think Earth retreated within the planet when we took Genarg?"

"Yes," Death said, nodding. "The Queen would see it as cowardly, but she doesn't respect Earth very much."

Hack nodded. "She comes rushing here, and we're waiting for her. Earth pops up to apologize, and the Queen dismisses him. Then, Earth kills the Queen, Death freezes her soul, and Sebastian cleanses her soul. We take her artifact container back to the station and destroy it."

"Fuck, we have a plan," Beck said, grinning.

"A good plan," Selene agreed.

"Don't get ahead of yourselves," Beol said, voice grim. "We would still need to take the planet."

Death smiled. "Oh, I think I could be of some help with that."

———

THEY WAITED UNTIL NIGHT FELL. EARTH ORDERED HER workers to the prisoner camp and insisted on handpicking the guards for the night.

Beck, Beol, and a few of the others had decided to stay on the planet while everyone else returned to the ships.

Beck sat at the edge of the pit, legs dangling over, and frowned. He really needed to stop calling it the pit.

"Earth, what do you call this? I've been thinking of it as the baby pit, but that sounds like we're tossing babies in pits."

Earth smiled. She sat next to him and Beol. "I call this one the Hollow. Two of my workers know and help me when I need it. We always say we're going to the Hollow."

"This one? You have more?" Leti's eyes widened, and Beck laughed.

"Six more for the Crell," Earth answered. "Hundreds more for all the animal species I will eventually bring back."

"That's gonna be a lot of babies," Beck said, trying to picture almost a hundred babies crawling around the jungle.

"How do your workers feel about this?" Beol waved to the piles of soil.

Earth hummed. "Surprisingly, the two that know are supportive. I speak with them often, and they understand my grief at the loss of my people. Many of my workers are transients with no homes of their own. The galaxy is a large and unforgiving place."

Beck thought about Brinanda. "I know. It's hard to

take sometimes. There's lots of good out there, but there's bad too."

Beol took his mate's hand in both of his and smoothed his fingers over Beck's fur. "I'm surprised your workers keep such a secret."

Earth grimaced. "I know what you mean. In each cycle, the workers are under my guardianship, and I do my best to take care of them. This cycle, they came here as prisoners, and the Concords treated them horribly. I took all of them that they brought, and I try to make their lives bearable."

"They're still slaves," Silas said bluntly.

"Yes," Earth nodded. "Until they're freed tonight. That will make them very happy. It will make me very happy."

"Why did you want to hand-pick the guards?" Beol studied Earth, and Beck wondered what he was thinking.

"There are some that treat my workers well. They feel pity for them."

"You want them spared?"

"If it's possible."

"I don't understand you," Maia said, shaking her head. "You stood aside every other cycle, but now you're suddenly kind and thoughtful?"

"There's a reason my Queen chose Life over me once she was resurrected," Earth said softly. "She respects power and cruelty. I build and create. I don't destroy."

"She does," Leti said quietly.

Earth was silent for a moment and stared up at the

night sky. "My Queen, my true Queen, would be appalled at what I allowed to happen. I chose to serve a monster instead of protecting her people."

"You loved her," Beck said. He took Earth's hand in his empty one.

"If I truly loved her, then I would have done what she wanted me to do," Earth said bitterly.

"You will this time," Sebastian said. "You'll finally free her from the cycle of resurrection and bring back the Crells."

"Yes, I will."

Beck's comm chimed, and he answered it.

"Okay," Clara said. "Our fleet is through the planetary defenses. We'll land after, uh, Death does his thing."

"He is not to touch those in my camp," Earth reminded her. "Neither the workers nor the guards."

"Got it," Clara said. "He'll start his thing in one hour. That gives you guys time to get to the camp."

"We'll head out now."

"Alber finished hacking the planet's defenses too. We'll have complete control by the time Death cleans up down there."

Beol gave her a grim smile. "Good job."

"Thanks, Clara," Beck said and ended the call. He slowly stood. "Let's get there and make sure people don't freak out."

Icarus helped Earth up, nibbling his lip. "Earth, would it be okay with you if I take one of those red flower plants home with me when we go? It's super pretty, and I'll take really good care of it. It could see the galaxy on the way back to Charybdis Station."

"Beck told me you have a fern named Fawn," Earth said, smiling. "If you will let me meet her, I'll help you transplant one of my flowers."

Earth and Icarus chatted about Genarg's flora and fauna all the way back to the temple. The camp was on the outskirts of the town, so it took the full hour for all of them to get there.

Two guards stood at the only gate in and out of the encampment. Both were human men.

"Earth." One of them stood at attention. "Who are these people? Are you alright?"

"Jon." Earth nodded to him. "All those I requested are here?"

"Yes, ma'am." He looked nervous. "I know you like us best, but if you request us too often, management will get suspicious."

Beol checked the time and winked at Beck. "Management isn't going to be around much longer."

Beck looked up when he noticed the soft glow. The guards and Earth raised their eyes as well.

Thousands of souls were slowly floating up from the town. They trickled through the sky, heading to where Beck knew the Blue Sparrow flew with the other ships.

"What's happening?" The other guard shivered. "Are those souls? Is that guy, Death, here?"

Earth laid a hand on the man's arm. "Yes, Raj. Genarg is allying with Charybdis Station now. Humans First will be expelled from my planet."

The two humans shared a defeated look. "I wish Captain Chynella hadn't signed up with them," Raj said. "Will running do any good?"

"No," Beol said. "Switching allegiance will. I'm the Guild Master of Half-Moon. Earth assures us you are worth saving."

"Half-Moon?" Jon's eyes widened, and he stifled a squeal.

Raj opened and closed his mouth, frozen with shock.

Beck grinned. They were fanboying over his mate. He started laughing.

Beol glared at him.

"Dad's guild is the best," Icarus said. "If you're nice, he might let you join."

"After you prove your loyalty," Sax said with a scowl. "What kind of assholes join Humans First?"

"The kind that didn't have a choice," Raj said, voice shaking as he watched the souls disappear. "If we wanted off Vextonar, we had to do something. Neither of us had any skills. We joined the first mercenary group that would take us."

"They just happened to be shitty," Jon said. "Captain Chynella chose to join Humans First, and the only way you leave her crew is by dying."

"Stage One's done. Now, Death and the planetary defenses will take out the ships around the planet," Beck said once the souls had disappeared.

Earth tilted her head. "I still sense some in the town."

"Death may have decided they weren't too bad,"

Beck said, shrugging. "I'm not sure what all he sees when he goes to take a soul."

Earth nodded. "Jon, will you and Raj please go into town and find the living? It will be disturbing, but they are likely scared."

"Sax and I will go too," Icarus said. "We can explain what's going on."

Beck grabbed his tail and grumbled, unhappy at the thought of his son doing something that risky.

Beol leaned up and kissed him. "I'll go with them, Sparky. I won't let anyone take our kids."

"Kids?" Sax arched a brow.

"You and Meggie are practically ours too," Beol said, shrugging. "Come on."

Beck watched them go until Meggie linked her arm in his.

"Let's go check on these folks, Beck. They're probably confused."

"I'm assuming it's all adults?" Leti walked with Earth into the camp.

The place was packed with small houses and a lot more people than Beck had expected.

"I took everyone the Concords brought so they wouldn't have to stay on the ships as playthings," Earth said. "There are many children and elders."

Leti made a strangled noise, and they all turned to look at him. His eyes were frozen on a young boy sitting on the steps of one of the houses. He was about four or five years old and a hybrid with blond hair and brown eyes. The boy looked miserable.

"That's Elril," Earth said. "His parents were killed by

the Concords before he arrived here. We do our best to care for him."

"He's just a little older than Sami," Leti said and rushed to the boy. "Hi, Elril. My name's Leti."

"Oh, fuck," Maia said. "He really doesn't have any parents?"

"No," Earth said sadly. "There are several children here who have no family left. We do our best to care for each other, but it's a group effort."

"Leti just adopted another kid, didn't he?" Silas grinned.

———

WHILE DEATH FROZE SHIPS ABOVE THE PLANET, AND Beol's assassin Alber shot them to pieces, Hack ran around the yard, Elril on his back. The boy held onto Hack's long pointed ears and giggled.

Leti carried a bowl of stew to one of the tables in the center of the encampment, Jenks buzzing around him in lazy circles. "You two settle down now. It's time for little boys to have their dinner."

Dru shook her head. "Gods, this makes five kids and three of Hack's siblings."

"You know they've been fucking like rabbits too," Morgan said. "How much you want to bet Leti announces he's preggo by the time we get back to the station?"

"I'll take that bet," Sebastian said. "Leti did *not* enjoy childbirth."

Beck ignored them, too distracted to add his own

wager. Beol sat on Beck's lap, softly petting the fur on his bare shoulder. It was a lot warmer on Genarg than it was on the station. Beck had decided a simple undershirt was better than his Blue Solace jacket.

Beol kissed his shoulder. "You're practically vibrating."

"I want to shift so bad," Beck said, shivering at the feel of his mate's lips. "There are so many things to explore here."

"Once the video is sent and you've eaten, you can go out," Beol said.

"Thank you, Guild Master," Beck said with a grin.

Beol bit his shoulder. "Don't sass me, Sparky."

When Beck saw Cordelia and Wyatt coming, he groaned and set Beol aside. "I have to go make that video."

"I'll make a plate for you." Beol kissed his cheek.

Beck hummed in pleasure before turning to his friend. "Hack, put your new son down and come on. We've got a video to make."

"Do we really have to do this right now?" Cordelia pulled on the collar of the pink blouse Wyatt had picked out for her.

"Yes," Wyatt said. "It needs to be breaking news, and a few of those ships that were off planet retreated, so you know the news will be out soon. Chin up and smile."

Cordelia growled. "I hate you."

Wyatt blew her a kiss, then sat in Morgan's lap. "Have fun now."

Hack had decided Cordelia would do the interview

since she was pretty and mostly human. They needed to make this look as convincing as possible.

When President Wineon had ordered the very likable reporter, Larry Sutton, executed, she had made an enemy of most media stations. A station on Vextonar had already agreed to show their video and spread it to other stations. They would do their part to piss off the Queen.

They left the prison encampment and hurried to the empty streets of the town.

"Alright, Cordy," Beck said. "We're recording in three, two, one."

Cordelia smiled wide and fluttered her eyes. *Damn, she looks weird when she acts preppy and flirty*, Beck thought.

"Hi, this is Cordy Blue standing in for Larry Sutton. I'm on the planet Genarg in the Crellic System. For over a year now, the media has covered the story of the Crellic Queen and her Elements. I'm here to investigate the rumor that the Queen has lost her homeworld and all of her Elements."

Beck moved the camera over the empty town, before moving back to Cordelia.

"As you can see, the streets of the only town on Genarg stand empty. Humans First recently held the planet, but General Hackett of Charybdis Station liberated the planet less than an hour ago."

Hack stepped into view and grinned. "Good evening, Ms. Blue."

Cordelia blushed and patted her hair. "Hello, General. I didn't realize you'd be so handsome. Oh, dear." She cleared her throat. "Can you tell me why you decided to take Genarg? It's of no importance to Humans First, and Charybdis Station has been very vocal about their disapproval of Humans First's philosophy."

"Honestly? We thought the Queen was more dangerous than HF, but we were clearly wrong."

"What do you mean? Wasn't it difficult to take Genarg?"

"Not at all," he said, shrugging. "The Queen wasn't here, and her Element Earth retreated into the planet to hide. Plus, we have the Element Death on our side. At this point, the Queen is superfluous. HF pulls her strings, and she basically belongs to them. Now, she has no real power of her own."

"Goodness," Cordelia said. "What will you do with Genarg now that it belongs to you?"

Hack grinned again. "I was thinking of settling down and making it my own. There's a lot of resources to drill out of this planet. I think I can make a credit or two before it's a barren rock again. It even comes with a comfy throne."

The interview went on for another five minutes, Cordelia and Hack doing their best to make the Queen sound like a useless idiot that was being manipulated by the geniuses of HF. They wrapped up and Beck looked back over the feed, tweaking a few things before sending it to Hack.

Hack took a breath. "I'll send this out. The station will polish it up, then send it around. Here's to hoping it pisses her off enough to bring her here."

"It will," Death said. "This hits her ego."

"She won't like being made to look a fool," Earth said. "This will work."

———

Three days later, Beol's comm woke Beck and his mate up. Beck curled around Beol and nuzzled the back of his neck.

"Yes? Ninetta?" Beol answered the comm, still half asleep.

The babies really do drain him, Beck thought.

"Boss-man, your video did the job," Ninetta said, voice shaking. "I listened in on their comm chatter. The four big bosses of HF ordered the Queen to stay the course and travel to Charybdis Station with Cortez's fleet."

"What did she say?"

"You know that thing Fire does? With the ships? Well, the Queen doesn't share his finesse. The reactors exploded in two-thirds of their ships, killing everyone on board and tearing the ships to pieces," Ninetta said. "After all the screaming, I heard the Queen ordering the surviving ships to head toward the Crellic System."

18

CRELLIC SYSTEM, PLANET GENARG -
TWO MONTHS LATER

*B*eol sat with Leti and Wolfe in the shade and watched Beck, Bloop, and Xav chase the children around the large vegetable garden in their shifted forms.

The prisoners had a total of twenty-three children under the age of sixteen. While most of those had families, many didn't. A few men and women from the Charybdis crews had adopted children, but there were still six orphans that would be heading back to Charybdis Station. Fasi was already finding them homes.

"I can't believe this place has changed so much in just a couple of months," Leti said.

"It's not a military town anymore," Beol said. "Earth and his workers have made it their own."

Surprisingly, very few of the former prisoners chose to leave Genarg. Beol supposed Earth had been right when he had said many didn't have homes anymore. The guards that Earth had hand-picked had all chosen to stay as well.

One of Haroon's soldiers had volunteered to fly those that wanted to leave out on one of the smaller empty merc ships. They had arrived at Derelict in the Boral System a few days ago.

The rest of the prisoners were now inhabitants of Genarg. They had moved into the town and claimed it.

"Earth cares about them," Leti said. "She really loves these people."

"You said he ruled beside the Queen, right? It makes sense he would make a good leader."

Beol smoothed his hand over his rounded belly. He was only five months along, but it seemed like he doubled in size each week. At least the morning sickness was gone. The belly didn't make his training any easier, and he still took way too many naps.

Tinker flew down and sprawled on his belly, pressing her ear against him. She hummed softly, a sweet and innocent tune.

Elril and a little girl squealed when Beck pounced on them and licked their faces.

Xav caught another two and playfully rolled over them. After a few minutes of fun, the smaller, lilac-colored Grell jumped up and took after the rest of the kids.

"I wonder what it would be like to shift," Leti said, shaking his head. He scratched Princess Buttercup's nose. The dragon sprawled beside Leti's chair with his head in Leti's lap.

Wolfe yawned. "We'll never know," he signed.

The three of them looked up when Jen jogged over to them. The reporter had arrived two weeks ago. Her news station wanted coverage on the battle with the Queen. Hack hadn't wanted to say no since the Vextonar Hotspot had been essential in getting the Queen to head this way.

Jen had volunteered, and the young human had brought friends. Six ships full of friends to be exact. The humans ranged from all ages and professions, but they all had one thing in common. They had each lost loved ones when President Wineon had *purged* the planet.

They wanted their pound of flesh and taking HF's favorite weapon away from them would do the job.

"Hey, Jen," Leti said. "You finished training with Selene?"

"That woman is a fiend," Jen said, collapsing to the grass in front of their chairs. "I've never worked so hard in my life."

"This battle won't be easy, and if we fail, every person on this planet will have to fight for their life," Beol said.

"I know." Jen sighed. "I need to survive to show the galaxy what happens. If she dies, they need to see it. They need to know Humans First is declawed. They're afraid to even help the planets Air and the Queen destroyed."

Sebastian hurried toward them. He was a couple of months farther into his pregnancy than Beol, but the man carried the weight of his baby bump well.

My belly is already almost as big as Sebastian's, Beol thought sourly.

"Remy is going to do his Rite of Passage tonight. You guys need to come and cheer him on."

"Damn," Leti said. "He's already doing it?"

Sebastian grinned proudly. "He could have done it a while ago, but we've all been distracted by the Queen, and he's been helping me train people. Jalyn will be ready soon too."

A few of Earth's people had decided they wanted to try to train in Crellic shamanism with Remy, Jalyn, and Sebastian. Earth had been ecstatic.

"We'll be there, Seb," Leti said. "Sit with us and gossip? Beol is a grumpy kitty, Wolfe won't tell me the good stuff he finds out, and Jen doesn't know the good stuff."

Beol growled half-heartedly. He really wished Icarus had never called him that. Now everyone was. "Here, take my seat, Sebastian. I need to go check on Rus."

Leti looked stricken. "We love you, Beol. You don't have to leave. I know you're not a grumpy kitty."

Beol slowly got up and ruffled Leti's hair. "I know you do. I just want to visit with my son a bit."

Sebastian took his seat, groaning. "Good. My feet hurt, and I need a break. Okay, so how are your kids taking to Elril?"

"Rizzie says I should pick one of the girls instead, like I'm shopping for babies," Leti said. "Sami and Pepper thoroughly approve, and the others are already planning on spoiling him rotten. Now, let's talk about Val and Death. I got more details out of Fire yesterday."

Beol left them to their gossip and walked toward the Hollow. Icarus had taken to spending a lot of time there with Earth, Juniper, and Fire.

The jungle was strangely quiet. Only the wind whistled through the trees. Beol wondered how many animals Earth planned to bring back.

"This ivy only needs about two or three hours of sun a day and keep it low heat." Earth stood with Icarus, Juniper, and Sax near the Hollow. A small potted plant with long strands of green and tiny white flowers stood at their feet.

Beol felt a bout of sadness when he noticed Icarus and Sax holding hands. He had a feeling Icarus would be spreading his wings soon.

Earth looked up. "Beol. It's a pleasure to see you today."

Beol tilted his head. Earth had a funny way about him. He was oddly formal but covered in dirt. His hair was full of tangles and small twigs and leaves.

"Hey," Beol said. "Rus, are you enjoying yourself?"

Icarus grinned. "Genarg is so different, Dad. I know most of the recorded species of flora and fauna, so this is all new. I love it."

Sax met his eyes and shrugged. "He's a plant dork. At least he's cute."

Beol smiled softly and shook his head.

"Plants are amazing, Sax, not dorky," Juniper said, playfully scowling at the Bracken.

Dr. Bloop and a shifted Beck ran into the clearing and circled them, tails wagging.

Earth grinned. "Did you come to check on the babies, Beck?"

Beck's deep bark echoed around the trees.

"Come along then." Earth walked to the Hollow, and Beck and Bloop followed.

"They do this every day," Icarus said. "Dad really likes being able to shift and run, doesn't he?"

"I wonder why he stays on Charybdis Station instead of going to Grellweir." Sax watched them go.

"His family," Icarus said immediately.

"His friends too," Juniper added. "Sometimes I think the Brackenstones are the heart of Charybdis Station."

Sax nodded. "I guess I get that. I just really like seeing him like this."

"Me too," Beol said. "I'll have to make sure he gets to a planet sometimes. Seeing and smelling the same stuff over and over is probably boring."

Beol watched Beck carefully wander through the piles of dirt. He would sniff at one, then another, and finally decide to curl up next to one particular pile. It was the same one each time.

Icarus helped Beol climb into the pit, and Beol sat next to his mate. Beck lay his head atop Beol's belly and wagged his tail.

What was it about this pile of dirt that called to his mate?

———

LATER THAT NIGHT, THEY GATHERED AT THE TOP OF THE temple. The throne was an ominous reminder that the Queen would be arriving within a few days. Ninetta continued to track the remains of Cortez's fleet as it headed toward Genarg.

Death stood with Sebastian and Remy. Everyone in the tiny town gathered around them in the throne room. Jen and her cameraman had a prime spot to record the ritual.

The two young shamans were shirtless, and Sebastian's tattoos were displayed for everyone to see. So was his heavy belly.

"Why did *I* have to take my shirt off?" Sebastian tried to cover his belly with his hands, but there was just a little too much of it.

"In solidarity," Remy said, nudging him with his shoulder. "They're recording this, and you feel sorry for my pale ass. Remember?"

"Thank you for coming to share this moment with Remy," Death said, voice carrying over the small crowd. "I've seen this ritual performed for ages. The purpose is to celebrate the awakening of a new shaman. It's also meant to be a beautiful moment of self-discovery for the shaman. Remy has agreed that Ms. Rally can film the rite but know that is a great gift. Don't take it lightly."

"We will now begin the rite of passage to determine Remy's affinities," Sebastian said. "Six items lie here in a circle – a withered vine for death, a small fern frond for earth, Remy's cat for life, a lit candle for fire, a small bowl of water for water, and a whistle for air."

"I really hope my affinity isn't air," Remy said, grumbling. "I don't want a whistle tattoo."

Sebastian shrugged. "Be happy it's not Hack's face."

Hack sniffed. "If only you were so lucky, Seb."

Death cleared his throat and gave them a look. "To begin, Remy must walk around the circle and touch each item. By doing this, he mentally and spiritually shows what he intends these items to symbolize."

Remy walked around the circle and touched each item, then sat in the middle, legs crossed. after that.

To Beol, it was just a blur of colors and light. He leaned into Beck and whispered, "Do you understand what's going on?"

Beck chuckled. "Nope. It was like this with Sebastian's rite of passage too. The end is a bit showy though."

Beol grunted in surprise when the withered vine slid across the floor to Remy. "I guess we shouldn't be so surprised that death is one of his affinities."

"Death is Remy's first element affinity," Sebastian announced for the crowd.

Potato slid across the floor, hissing as he went. The cat calmed down when he reached his person and lay his head on Remy's knee.

"Life is his second affinity."

"Life and death," Death said. "That is… unusual."

Finally, the frond slid across the floor and settled at Remy's back.

"Earth is his third and final affinity," Death said. "Now, the elements will mark him."

The colorful threads of Remy's elements snaked

around his torso. Beol swore he could almost hear the threads singing.

With a burst of light, the threads sank into Remy's body, and the man cried out in pain. His eyes popped open and everyone gasped. Where Remy's eyes were normally blue, at that moment, they were completely black, just like Death's.

"Um, that didn't happen with Sebastian," Beck whispered harshly.

When the light cleared, Beol could see Remy's eyes were blue again, and the man's new shaman tattoos glowed slightly. The withered vine covered one shoulder while a very feline outline covered the other. Remy turned around, and Beol saw that the delicate frond covered his back.

Earth clapped, completely delighted. "You're one of mine. How wonderful."

They lined up to congratulate Remy, then afterwards, they headed to the food table. Beol found himself constantly hungry nowadays. He piled his plate high, then he and Beck sat with Icarus, Meggie, and Sax. The Bracken might not eat, but they enjoyed talking to people.

"Beck, I need some of those jumpy boots," Meggie said. "I want them in black, and if you can make them heels, that would be great."

"Oh, what are jumpy boots? I love shoes." Jen sat next to Meggie. The two women had become very good friends.

"They aren't jumpy boots," Beck said, grumbling. "They're altered gravitational hover boots."

Meggie gave him a dry look. "Why not just call them hover boots?"

Beck looked flustered. "Because they alter gravitational force."

"You really need to work on your marketing," Jen said.

"Anyway," Meggie said with an eye-roll, "I want a pair."

"That's fine. I have an extra pair with me, and I'll hook them up to your neuro-control implant. They aren't heels, but they should fit. I meant them to go to Selene. Why the hell would you want to jump in heels? Do you know how hard it'll be to land?"

Meggie shrugged. "Make them tonight. I want to wear them when the Queen arrives, and I'll need time to practice."

"Why do you want them?" Beol gave her a suspicious look.

She smiled sweetly. "I'm a medic, Beol. I need to move fast sometimes."

This girl is too good a liar, Beol thought. He didn't know for certain whether she was telling the truth or not.

Dannol brought his own plate and sat next to Meggie. The Havenite was short and slender to Meggie's tall and full-figured. "Hey, Megs."

Beck glared at him. "Dannol."

Dannol attempted to glare too. "Beck." The young pilot couldn't stick the finish and started giggling.

Meggie kicked Beck under the table. "You need to stop being mad at Dannol."

"He knew you two were mates and didn't tell you right away," Beck said, frowning. "It upset you."

Dannol leaned up and kissed Meggie, running his hand through her blue hair. "He's right. I really should have just told you. I wanted to give you time to enjoy life before you tied yourself to me and Nessa."

Dannol's adopted daughter was home on Charybdis Station. From all accounts, she adored Meggie, and the two talked every day.

"You can't help you're an idiot sometimes," Meggie said. "Beck can learn to let it go. We're together now, and Nessa knows I love her."

Icarus and Sax shared a sweet look, and Beol scowled. It was bad enough Meggie was moving on with Dannol, but he suspected Rus and Sax would be starting their own family soon.

"Dads, what would you two think of being grandfathers?" Icarus's hopeful look was enough to make Beol mind his tongue. He really didn't want to be Grandpa Beol. He was only thirty-two, damn it.

"What are you thinking of doing?" Beck sat forward with an eager look. "I could make another Bracken for you two."

Sax snorted. "You just want a reason to make another. No, Icarus and I were thinking of taking on one of the orphans here. We'd have to wait until we got citizenship."

"That's some bullshit right there," Jen said, angry. "You three shouldn't have to have the galaxy agree to treat you as a person before you can be a person. You *are* a person."

"Agreed," Meggie said and nudged her friend with her shoulder, smiling.

"I already told Grandma," Icarus said. "She's planting seeds in the Lord Admiral's ear. Those were her words, not mine."

Beck looked happy, then his eyes dimmed. "I guess you'll be moving out."

Beol couldn't stand the sadness in Beck's eyes. "Next door," Beol said briskly. "The house next door is empty and has three bedrooms. Bendix is on the other side of it, and Otto and Pris are behind it. You'll be protected."

Icarus beamed. "Really? We can live there?"

"It's either there or with us," Beol said, bluntly. "Those are your choices."

Sax smirked at him. "The grumpy kitty loves us."

———

LATER THAT NIGHT, BEOL LAY IN BED WITH BECK ABOARD the Blue Solace. He stroked Beck's fuzzy chest. "I love your fur. It's so soft."

Beck gave him a solemn look. "I'm glad. I'd hate to have to shave my whole body every day."

Beol grinned. "You would really do that?"

Beck would look so weird, but Beol would still love him. Well, maybe. He *really* liked his fur.

"Of course not," Beck said, laughing. "Do you know how long that would take?" He stilled after a moment and cupped Beol's face in his hands. "Are you happy with me, Beol?"

Beol smiled softly. "More than I ever thought I could be. My face hurts from smiling so much, Sparky."

"Even though we're here, away from your guild?"

"I've left them on missions before," Beol said. "Bendix is annoying, but also competent."

"It hasn't been easy, dealing with the Council about my boy."

"You mean *our* boy," Beol corrected. "Icarus is so much like you that I couldn't help but love him too."

"I can't promise to stop making Fyrlings and Bracken," Beck said. "Each one is just so rare, like a delicious toma fruit from Siren's Lament. Each one is shaped different and has a slightly different taste, but they're all yummy."

"You're making me hungry," Beol said. "I don't mind more Bracken, Sparky. The moment I knew your secret, I knew creating and inventing were a part of you, and I want every single part of you."

Beck grinned widely, looking so smugly happy Beol wanted to laugh.

Beck rolled Beol over onto his back and nuzzled his belly. "Our little ones are growing well, huh?"

"That's what Meggie and Nettle say."

"Are you really mad at the babies? I know it hasn't been easy carrying them."

Beol stroked Beck's black hair back from his forehead. "I already love them beyond belief. I'm just scared."

"You're gonna be a good dad, Beol."

Beol closed his eyes. "I hope so."

"You're not like your mom or your dad. You're like Hay."

"That would be... That would be a good thing. To be like Hay."

Beck pressed a kiss to his stomach and slowly undressed him, kissing every bit of skin he revealed. His mouth made a trail of hot, wet kisses to Beol's hard dick before sucking the tip.

Beol groaned and reveled in the feel of his mate's mouth, letting sensation carry him away.

19

A few days later, Beck looked around the workshop one more time before making the call.

Bloop and Tinker were with Beol, and Rus and the girls were with Earth. The Queen would arrive soon, and everyone was preparing. It was the first chance he'd gotten to be alone in a while. Not that he was complaining.

"Beckie Boo! Oh, it's so good to see your face." Ma's familiarity tugged at Beck's stomach. He liked sniffing around Genarg, but he missed home more.

"We're fighting the Queen soon."

"You'll do fine, son." Pops's face appeared beside Ma's. "You have your bots, right? Don't forget those boots of yours."

"Always bring an extra phaser, sweetie," Ma said.

"I will," he promised. "I just wanted to see you before it started. How's Nala doing?"

Ma rolled her eyes, but Pops grinned and said,

"She's doing just fine. I think she's the only housewife who's training with the soldiers though. She wants to be prepared just in case anyone comes after the Bracken again."

"Oh, speaking of the Bracken," Ma said. "I talked with Jalina yesterday. They've decided on a new Council member. Holli is Fallon and a close friend of the Prime Minister of Fallow. She's young, but Jalina said they needed that energy."

"The first order of business will be voting on the Bracken's citizenship," Pops said. "By the time you get back, I bet Fasi will have arranged for Sax and Icarus to adopt. It's happening, son. I wish it hadn't taken so long."

"It would have taken years anywhere else," Beck said. He might still be sore about Brinanda's betrayal, but he knew Charybdis Station was special. He shook himself. "Okay. We'll do this, then I'll call you guys right away. Tell my horrible sisters I love them. Oh, and tell Jyra to stop calling Beol to tell stories about me. It's rude."

Ma's smile was full of love and worry both. "We love you all so much. I'm going to call Beol and Icarus now, so they're not distracted later. We'll talk to you soon."

The call ended, and Beck sucked in a breath. He put his neuro-control implant on and checked his bots over. He'd added two more since leaving home. He'd upgraded his bubble bot too. If he could get close enough to the Queen to cut her, she'd feel it.

He left the ship and headed for the bar. He and

Alber had set up a control room in one of the rooms above the bar.

Alber was one of Half-Moon's IT engineers and came highly recommended by Hay. The assassin was quiet, but friendly.

"Planetary defenses are as good as I can make them," Alber told Beck when he walked in. "I don't think they'll be able to hack them."

"They won't need to," Beck said, sighing. "She'll just ignite the wiring inside of the satellites, then it's all gone."

"Our fleet will be waiting on them when they enter the atmosphere," Alber reminded him. They had twenty-two ships total. That was taking into account their own five, the six from Vextonar, and the eleven that had been docked on the planet when they'd taken it. Dannol, Linc, and the other pilots would do their damnedest to take out the Queen's small fleet.

"They're shielded, and that will be an advantage, but you know ships will get by them. Ninetta said the Queen had almost forty.

"We have the pulse cannons around the town," Alber said. "The volunteers and I will be manning them. We'll try to take as many ships out as we can when they try to land."

Beck rubbed his face. "We'll be waiting for them on the ground, and everyone will have several injectors. Jon and the other former guards will be hidden in the Hollow with the civilians and our pets. If it comes to it, they'll try to get them out of there."

Beck thought of the little Crell he curled next to

every day. They were innocent and had an important future ahead of them.

"Beck, this is the best plan we have," Alber said. "Honestly, it's a much better plan than we started with."

"You're right."

"It's getting late. The Guild Master is probably looking for you."

Beck smiled. "Are you trying to get rid of me?"

Alber grinned. "Yeah. You're stressing me out."

Beck slapped him on the back and left, heading toward the temple. They had no idea where the Queen would land, but the temple was the highest structure. They'd be able to see things better from there.

Beol sat on the steps at the front. He wore black body armor and was covered in weapons. His own little bot circled above his head.

Beck sat next to him and pulled his mate into his arms. "You'll be careful, right?"

"Yes. I'll do my best not to take chances. I have a feeling Death, Fire, and Sebastian are going to be her focus."

"Sebastian is seven months pregnant," Beck said. "I can't believe he's doing this."

"Alois isn't happy."

Icarus and Sax found their way to them and sat. They each had three bots circling them.

"Ms. Rally is at the top of the temple with her cameramen," Icarus said, wrapping an arm around Sax. "Earth went to ground. She'll stay in her Element form until the Queen arrives."

"Meggie is having sex with Dannol," Sax said, then

sighed. "I think it's the danger. Hack and Leti were going at it in one of the shuttles."

"Did you really need to tell us that?" Beck grimaced.

Sax shrugged, but Beck recognized that mischievous look in her eyes.

"You two be careful today. You may be stronger and tougher than us, but you can still hurt and be destroyed," Beol said.

Beck took Icarus's hand in his. "Don't be like Leti's Icarus, okay?"

His son made a face. "I'm not flying too close to the sun. How was that even possible anyway? It gets colder in the upper atmosphere."

"Don't argue," Beck said with a laugh. "Just don't go crazy."

Slowly, Beck's friends gathered on the steps. Selene sat behind him and leaned her arms on his shoulders. Her bots circled over her head.

Hack and Leti cuddled together nearby. Princess Buttercup was massive, around twenty-feet long and five-feet wide. He was clearly ready to kick some ass.

Wyatt and Morgan sat together and spoke softly with Death. Beck knew Wyatt was afraid for his father. Death would be a prime target for the Queen.

Sebastian sat squished between Alois and Fire. Both men were worried about Sebastian. Hell, Beck was worried about him. He would be shielded, but a shield could only take so much, and the Queen could see them anyway.

Dru and Lerais sat with the rest of the Blue

Sparrow crew. Monty perched on Dru's shoulder. As usual, the vexal newt was going into battle with her.

Cordelia and Quinn held hands and chatted with Hazel and Linc.

Xav and Haroon sat with their crews and the rest of the Half-Moon assassins. The two men were arguing with Moyra about who the best captain was.

Beck was watching Silas and Rune snuggle when he noticed Tinker buzzing toward them. The Fyrling shook her fist at them and chattered angrily.

"Tinker, you're supposed to be with Bloop," Beol said, frowning.

Beck had left Bloop curled up next to his favorite pile of dirt with Gravy and Elril.

She ignored Beol and sat on his shoulder.

"I think she wants to fight too," Dru said. "Monty's like that."

"Damn it, Tinker," Beol said.

The Fyrling left his shoulder and spread out over his belly, humming happily.

Beck took a breath and let it out, trying to relax. The hardest part of any battle really was the waiting.

———

THEY CAME AT DUSK.

Just as Beck thought, the Queen sparked fires in the wiring of the satellites, and the planetary defenses went dead.

They activated their shields and waited as the Queen's fleet was picked off by unseen ships. Beck almost felt sorry for them. All their systems read clear air, then a missile would hit them from close by, pushing through their shields. After that, they were just pieces falling to the ground.

One of their borrowed ships suddenly appeared in the sky, its shield shorting out. Beck could see it smoking from where he stood. A small, non-descript ship spiraled away from it, and their ship crashed to the right of town.

Beck hoped there were survivors.

"The Queen can see the ships," Death said. "Luckily, I think her line of sight is limited or we'd be losing all of them."

Two more of their ships lost their shielding, then crashed to the ground. Beck tried to keep his eyes on the small ship, but things got chaotic as some of the Queen's fleet made it through. Each one headed straight for the town.

Alber and the volunteers powered up their pulse cannons, firing as many shots toward the ships as they could. Beck wanted to cheer when one, then two, then three ships burst into flames and fell to the ground.

Despite the cannons, several ships landed at the edge of town, doors opening and soldiers pouring out. Haroon, Xav, and Moyra's crews slid forward, unseen, to meet them. Beol squeezed Beck's hand, then disappeared.

Beck forced himself to focus and not grab his tail and whine. His mate could take care of himself.

HF wasn't faring well. One man ran toward the temple, rifle raised high, only to find himself stabbed from behind. They couldn't fight what they couldn't see. Unfortunately, there were far too many. The central street quickly filled with soldiers.

"Time to go, Princess." Beck heard Leti's voice, but he didn't see them. He felt the buffets of air as Princess took to the sky carrying Leti and Maia.

Leti's voice came through the comm unit in his ear. *"Those in the street in front of the bar, Princess is coming through in five, four, three, two, one."*

A loud roar shook the windows of the nearby houses, and a wave of fire crashed through the HF soldiers on the ground.

"Oh, listen to those screams," Hack said joyfully.

Alber's voice came over the comm. *"Leti, can you and Princess help us near the edge of town? We're getting overrun."*

"We're on our way."

A group of soldiers started up the stairs of the temple, drawing their attention away from the fighting in the streets.

Beck focused and his bots started firing on the soldiers. With eight bots having impeccable aim, the enemy soldiers' shields went down fast.

He tossed one of his electric-grenade prototypes, and bolts of electricity shot through the soldiers, frying them quickly.

As Hack, Selene, and the others blocked off another group of soldiers, something caught his eye. Beck looked up from the fight. Night had fallen, and the Queen's fleet was mostly grounded, one way or another, but one small ship circled above them. It was smoking, so it looked like it could be crashing, but it was too controlled.

He spoke into his comm. *"Hack, there's a suspicious ship up above. I think it might be the Queen."*

Death's voice was ominous as it came through. *"She's here."*

"Let's say hello then." Beck didn't recognize the voice, but one of the volunteers stationed on top of the closest house fired shot after shot from his pulse cannon into the ship.

More pulse cannon shots hit the ship from the other volunteers, and the ship dived toward the temple. Everyone moved as fast as they could to stay out of the way as it crashed near the top of the steps.

Less than a minute later, the side of the ship exploded outward, slinging metal toward them. Beck barely dodged a massive piece but fell when something whipped past his leg, slicing into him.

He lay still for a minute and stared at the ship. The Queen wasn't a thing like her golem. He could feel her rage, even as far away as he was. She stood tall and horrifically beautiful, pink skin glittering in the lights from the temple.

She started down the steps, face twisted in anger. "Genarg is my planet. Mine!"

Beck felt a zip of electricity fire through him. His shield deactivated and sizzled on his wrist. He looked around. All of their shields were gone.

He held his phaser up, and it was still charged. At least there was that.

Death watched her silently, black eyes focused

entirely on her. She stopped moving and turned her head to glare at him. Beck knew it would take all of the man's concentration to hold her still.

Moyra, Silas, and Juniper stood guard over him.

"Traitor. As if I need to move to destroy your friends. I'll enjoy killing this Wyatt I've heard so much about."

She turned to look out at them as they fought the soldiers.

"I am the Queen of the Crells, and you will serve me or die." As she spoke, the ground behind them trembled and rolled.

The paved road cracked and hundreds of large, human-like figures climbed out. They were rock, soil, and fire. One grabbed the nearest person, an HF soldier, and picked him up, rumbling as it ripped the man apart.

The rock monsters tromped toward them, tearing through anyone in their way, friend or foe.

Earth rose from the ground near him, naked body covered in mud. Her tortured eyes went straight to the Queen.

"My Queen," she said and rushed up the stairs.

"My precious coward," the Queen sneered. "Finally showing your face?"

The rock creatures lumbered closer.

"Fuck," Cordelia said. She crouched beside him. "Come on, Beck. Get up."

"My leg." He tried to stand, but the flesh on his left leg was split open in several spots.

Cordelia wrapped an arm around his waist and heaved until he was on his feet.

"Serve or die!" Slender funnels of air formed on either side of the Queen and Earth, twisting into two small but deadly landspouts. The skies darkened and thunder rumbled as wind whipped through the town.

"Whoa, almost fell off Princess. What was that?"

Hack's panicked voice came through on the comm. *"The skies aren't safe, baby. Get on the ground."*

Wind tore through the streets, and they were blown down the steps of the temple, toward the rock creatures.

Beck cried out as his leg hit the stone steps over and over again.

He heard Cordelia's head thump hard against one as she tumbled with him, groaning.

"Cordy?"

She moaned but didn't move.

The landspouts doubled, splitting into four slender funnels before shooting out toward Beck and the others.

Jalyn darted forward and held her hands up, squeezing her eyes shut and focusing. She glowed brightly, and the landspouts stopped moving forward, twisting and turning in place.

The Queen laughed. "More baby shamans to kill. How lovely."

Sebastian struggled against the wind to stand beside Jalyn, his eyes focused on the landspouts, and he raised his hands too. Slowly, they turned and headed back toward the crashed ship.

The Queen's laughter turned to angry shrieks, and the landspouts burst into flamespouts, breaking from Jalyn and Sebastian's hold and shooting back toward the two shamans.

"You can't hurt Sebby!" Fire disappeared into his Elemental form, his clothes burning to a crisp. Wild rings of flame circled Sebastian, and Beck could see the outline of the tattoo on his back through his shirt. It was pulsing with life, much like Hack's did when he channeled his inner fire.

Sebastian's mouth dropped open as his whole body began to glow with a fiery light. He shook his head.

"Okay, buddy. I get it. *You're* fire. Let's do this."

Mustachio soared over the battle, trilling a song that seemed to soothe and focus Sebastian.

A wall of fire sprung up between them and the Queen, engulfing the flamespouts. It spread out until it completely circled the Queen.

"Fire is mine to control," she screamed, and the flames wavered, moving toward Sebastian.

"Fire belongs to himself," Sebastian yelled. "He is a free Element, and you will never rule him again. You've lost your right to the Elements."

Beck could almost feel the joy in the flames as the wall solidified and pushed toward the Queen.

Alois, Beol, and Wolfe moved to stand around Jalyn and Sebastian as HF soldiers ran toward them, intent on killing them.

Icarus and Sax cut the attackers off, tearing through them with phasers and blades. The two Bracken moved faster than anything Beck had seen before, twisting and turning with beautiful efficiency.

"Fuck," Cordelia said, drawing his attention. She stood, shaking her head.

The rock monsters were close. They moved slowly, but nothing seemed to stop them. They had torn through several groups of HF soldiers, finally reaching Beck and his friends.

Cordelia and Beck fired into them.

"Phasers aren't doing shit," Morgan said from their right.

A shot from a pulse cannon came from the house on their left, blasting into one of the monsters. Bits of dirt sprayed over all of them. *I'll do what I can, but there's a lot of them, and the others are focused on the bulk of the soldiers in town.*

Beck pulled one of his electric grenade prototypes out and threw it toward one of the monsters. It hit the creature directly in the chest and electricity shot through it. Nothing.

He saw Selene toss a frag grenade and hit the same creature in the shoulder. The grenade detonated, and the creature exploded into dirt and rock.

"Use the frag grenades," Selene called out and tossed another one.

One of her bots swirled over the rock monsters, dropping frag grenades atop them. *It would run out eventually,* Beck thought. They would all run out of grenades eventually.

A pulse blast took out another one.

The ground shook and more of the creatures crawled out.

"Damn it!" Morgan yelled.

Beck almost laughed and sobbed both when he saw Tinker fly over the creatures and drop a grenade before zipping back to Beol for another.

Beck focused his bubble bot, and it shot toward the closest creature, spinning with blades and bubbles.

It took a minute, but the blades cut through, slicing the creature to pieces.

"Blades work too," he called out.

He looked at Cordelia. "Go! I'll use my bots, Cordy. You have to take care of yourself."

"Fuck that."

"Cordelia," he said firmly. "You have to help kill those creatures."

Hack ran by, shooting a wave of fire toward one of the monsters. It didn't faze it at all. "It's just blades and grenades, everyone. Hop to it."

Icarus and Sax attacked one, tag-teaming it. They sliced it to pieces and moved to another.

"Cordelia, I'll be okay."

Before he could say more, one of the creatures reached them and grabbed Cordelia's arm. She screamed as it pulled her up, snapping her arm like a twig.

Beck focused. His bot flew through, spinning its blades directly through the creature's chest.

Cordelia dropped, the bone in her arm poking out.

"Cordelia," he said, then focused his bot as another creature appeared.

Suddenly, Meggie was landing from a long jump. "Boots work good, Beck."

She quickly bound Cordelia's arm while Beck's bot sliced through another creature. She knelt beside him and applied something to his leg before wrapping it.

"I'll be back for you, Beck."

"No. Work on others. I'll be okay with my bots."

Several wounded and dead lay around them. Hazel's empty eyes stared at him from where she lay, torn to pieces by the rock creatures.

"I understand," she said softly. "I've already carried Lerais and Dru both to safety."

She picked Cordelia up easily and jumped again, disappearing into the night sky.

Beck focused his bots on the monsters, taking out another one. He really should have had more than two with blades.

Sebastian and Fire's wall of flames pressed closer to the Queen and Earth. The Queen called her own flames, pushing back against the wall.

Beck searched around for Death. The Element stood with Remy and watched Fire swirling around Sebastian with something like awe on his face. He leaned over and whispered in Remy's ear, then grabbed his hand, linking their fingers. Remy's eyes went black, and he looked out toward the battle field.

A pulse poured from him, and the dead HF soldiers slowly rose to their feet, life animating them, even as their eyes remained empty.

"Gods. I thought Death said that wasn't possible." Beck watched as the reanimated dead attacked their fellow soldiers and the rock creatures. They shrugged off shots and lost limbs, tearing through the enemy with a frantic efficiency.

Soon enough, the only attackers left were a few rock creatures.

"Quinn," Morgan cried out, rushing to the fallen woman.

She clutched her shoulder and yelped when Meggie landed beside them and checked Quinn over.

Beck focused his bot and cut through the creature ambling toward them.

A screech filled the air and more rock creatures crawled from the ground. Remy tilted his head, then turned his eyes to them and focused on the Queen's creations. Death stood frozen, eyes closed as he clutched Remy's hand.

A dark light surrounded Remy, then the monsters crumbled to bits as the life drained from them.

More immediately rose, these with wings. Again, Remy destroyed them. More rose. More were destroyed.

Meggie finished treating Quinn, then picked her up and jumped away.

Beck stared through the wall of fire. The Queen would keep summoning creatures again and again until Remy and Death tired out. She'd probably do the same with Sebastian and Fire.

They needed to kill her now while she was distracted by both Elements. He didn't know why Earth hesitated. Well he *did* know why she hesitated, but they needed to deal with this before the Queen stopped caring about destroying her own temple and planet.

Also, before the injector's case melted within the fire. He had done his best to fire and waterproof every single injector, but these weren't exactly normal flames.

If I can get over the wall with my boots, he thought, trying to stand. He sent a bot over the flames and saw it sizzle and disappear. Either the flames or the Queen had gotten it.

"Sparky." Beol was suddenly at his side, arm wrapping around his waist. "Damn it. You weren't supposed to get hurt."

Tinker cooed worriedly and patted Beck's face.

"Remy and Death are holding off the rock things, and Fire and Sebastian have her pinned," Beck said. "I need over that damn wall."

"Dad," Icarus said, running up to his other side. "Are you alright?"

Meggie was suddenly there. "Ready to go, Beckie Boo?"

"No, damn it. I need over that wall."

The ground trembled under them, and everyone fell to their knees as a physical wave of pressure spread out across the whole town. The walls of the buildings near them shuddered, and Beck saw the human that had helped them so much slide off his roof, landing unceremoniously in the bushes growing at the front of the house.

Beck peered through the flames. The Queen held Earth off her feet by her neck. Earth's feet kicked furiously, but to no avail. She sobbed in pain as flames raced up her body, the Queen no longer protecting her from them.

"YOU DARE BETRAY ME!"

"I need over that wall now," Beck said, struggling to stand on his wounded leg. "Earth's been found out."

"It's the only thing keeping her own fire from us," Beol argued.

"She has to die," Meggie said. She pulled an injector out of her pants pocket and jumped over Fire and Sebastian's wall of flame.

"Meggie!" Beck cried out.

20

"No," Beol whispered, eyes wide.

He could see Meggie through the flames. She screamed as she landed, body burning. Somehow, her arm lifted up.

Her hair, clothes, and skin burned, and she wailed in pain. For the first time, Beol wished the Bracken didn't have the ability to feel.

Meggie's arm lowered as she fell to her knees. Seconds later, the Queen's flames went out, and the rock monsters stayed piles of dirt.

Remy breathed out, and the animated corpses fell to the ground.

Sebastian lowered his arms, and the wall of flames disappeared. A thick ring of molten rock sizzled in the wall's place, burnt deep into the stone steps. Sebastian breathed heavily, and Fire still swirled around him in his Elemental form. "Jalyn, can you cleanse her soul? I don't think I have the energy."

Death held his hand out, pinning a vile green, black, and brown soul in the air. "Hurry, please."

Jalyn swallowed and closed her eyes, a glow surrounding her.

Beol didn't give a damn about the Queen or her soul.

Beck looked at him, eyes full of agony. "Meggie? Is she… Is she gone, Beol?"

"She can't be."

Beol's heart thundered as he ran toward Meggie. He stopped short when he came to the bubbling rock where Fire and Sebastian's wall used to be. It was over ten feet across and he didn't think he could jump it. Damn it.

"I'm up above, Beol. Princess will pick up Meggie and Earth. The center of the circle is still too hot even if you could get over that ring." Leti's voice was a small relief. Someone else was thinking about Meggie too.

Princess Buttercup dipped down and gently picked up Meggie's smoking body in one hand and Earth's rapidly healing body in the other.

Beol ran back down the steps to Beck. His poor mate was pale and in a lot of pain. Princess set Earth and Meggie down, and Beck crawled to Meggie.

She twitched as they watched her. Her skin was burnt away, and the metal of her frame was completely visible. Her face and her legs were twisted and melted.

"Meggie?" Beck's voice was broken. "Meggie girl, please be okay. I don't have my scanner. Why didn't I bring my scanner?"

"I'll scan her, Dad." Icarus hugged his father and

looked Meggie over. "Her core isn't too hot, and her frame is mostly complete. Some circuits and sensors are burnt out. Unfortunately, her voice is one of them."

Icarus hugged Beck and pulled Beol close. "She's still in there, Dads. We can fix her up, okay?"

Dannol ran up the street with Alber and the other volunteers. "Meggie!"

Sax caught him in her arms before he could touch the hot metal of Meggie's frame. "She's still alive, Dannol, but she needs a lot of work. Beck will fix her up. It'll just take time."

Meggie's arm lifted toward Dannol, and he reached out, trying to take her hand.

Sax pulled him back. "We'll get you a pair of those gloves of Beck's so you won't burn yourself. Let's just sit right here and talk to her. We need to let her know she's not alone."

Beck sobbed and crawled closer to her. "We're here, Meggie, and I'm going to fix you up. You killed the Queen, Meggie. You and those damn jumpy boots."

"I'm sorry, Meggie," Earth whispered from nearby. Her body was almost completely healed from the burns, but her hair was still gone, burnt off by the Queen's flames. "I hesitated, and she saw me try to inject her. I'm so sorry."

Icarus stood and picked Meggie up, bringing her to the rest of them. "It's okay, Earth. We know you loved her, and it was a hard thing you tried to do."

Selene sat with Beck and Icarus. She had some injuries, but nothing major.

"The Queen's soul is cleansed," Death said, sitting

next to them in the grass. He ignored the heat of Meggie's metal frame and took her hand in his. His flesh sizzled as it burned, but his expression stayed clear.

"Thank you, Meggie. Thank you for what you did. Beck *will* fix you, and we'll get you home to your new daughter."

Beol released a breath he hadn't realized he'd been holding. The lively, annoying girl he loved would be alright. Eventually.

"Death, what happened with Sebastian and Fire, then you and Remy?"

Death looked up. "Fire shares a very deep bond with Sebastian, far deeper than the bond he had with the Queen. In our first lives, we let her wield us, and it gave her immense power. Fire granted that gift to Sebastian."

"You and Remy?"

"We share a connection too, through his resurrection. I seldom let the Queen wield my power, but frankly, Remy is special. Life, death, and earth are very powerful affinities. I didn't even know what he did today was possible."

Beol looked around, then used his comm to check in. Wyatt, Rune, and Nettle worked with the other doctors and medics to treat the wounded. The five crews that had fought at the temple had several casualties and even more severe injuries.

Alois held Sebastian and a naked Fire in his arms, rocking both of them. Jalyn stood over them with

Wolfe. His brother had to practically carry her. She was completely drained.

Morgan sat beside Hazel's body and held her hand, and Moyra crouched beside him, hand on his shoulder.

Noe and most of the others in his guild were alive, though Noe had a bad head injury. Three of his people hadn't been so lucky. One was Clara. She had died fighting against one of the rock creatures.

Hack ran around the battleground, barking orders into his com and checking on his people. "We lost Hazel, Haroon lost two crewmembers, and Xav lost four. Damn it."

"Guild Master," Alber said, carefully lowering himself to his knees, "about a fourth of the human volunteers are dead, some in the crashed ships and some to the fighting once the soldiers landed. To be honest, I can't believe so many of us survived."

Beol watched as the human that had helped them with the rock creatures climbed out of the bushes he had fallen into. "We had a good plan and some very angry people fighting with us." Beol pulled Beck against him, settling his head on his mate's shoulder.

"Have you heard from Ninetta?"

"She jumped in to help the air battle. Last I heard, she was landing and helping with the injured."

The town lay in ruins. Between the crashed ships, the Queen's power, and the pulse cannons, most of the houses and buildings were falling down.

"We need to check on the civilians," Beck said hoarsely. "I don't know if anyone told them the Queen's dead."

"I'll go," Alber said, standing.

"Will you check on Bloop too?" Beol knew Tinker was safe. She currently buzzed around Earth, chattering sympathetically.

"Will do," Alber said and ran toward the jungle.

"You can go check on Half-Moon, Beol," Beck said. "I know you need to."

"I need to be with my mate," Beol said.

"We're okay," Beck said. "Once Meggie's body cools, we'll get her to the ship. Someone will tend my leg, and I'll be sleeping with Bloop before you know it."

"I'll take care of him, Dad," Icarus told Beol. "Clara didn't make it. You know that, right? Sax and I tried to get there in time. I think we all need jumpy boots."

Beol let the sadness well up for a moment before shoving it down. "I'll go check on them. Take care of our engineer, okay?"

———

SEVERAL HOURS LATER, BEOL AND TINKER MADE IT BACK to the Blue Solace. It was in one piece, thankfully. The engineering bay was quiet as they entered.

Meggie lay stretched out on a table, and Dannol sat on a cot next to her. The pilot looked up when Beol stepped in.

"How is she doing?"

"Beck already fixed the melted circuits and wiring. He said she looks worse than she actually is. Her face, legs, hips, and one of her arms are pretty mangled. He'll fix her up though."

"She can talk again?"

"Yes, grumpy kitty. I don't have lips, but I can talk again. I know you missed my voice," Meggie said, turning her head.

Beol felt his eyes fill with tears. He tried to stop them from falling. He very seldom cried and hated it. His tears didn't care. They fell down his cheeks, and a big sob made his body shake.

Dannol watched him in surprise, before jumping up and dragging Beol to the cot to sit.

"Don't you ever do that crazy shit again, Meggie," Beol finally managed to say. "I love you, Sax, and my Icarus too damn much."

Meggie held her hand out for him to hold. "Believe it or not, I really didn't want to do that. I don't want to leave you guys. I still have to technically meet Nessa."

Dannol hugged him tightly. "How are your people? Everybody is torn up about losing folks."

"We'll bury my three tomorrow. The others will be shipped home to their families." Beol barely recognized the sad voice as his own. "Sax and Icarus are working with the civilians to clean up what they can. Wyatt, Nettle, and all the rest of medical are still working to save people."

"It was a close call with Lerais," Dannol said. "Silas, Juniper, and Dru were all injured badly too. They'll make it though."

"Jen told me she recorded you, Meggie," Beol said, smiling sadly. "You saved so many people jumping in and out of the battle."

"She came by earlier," Meggie said. "I wouldn't let

her video me." She ran a head over her head. "I'm hideous."

"You're fucking beautiful," Dannol and Beol said at the same time.

"Geez, guys. I get it." Meggie's voice held a laugh. "How's Earth?"

Dannol gave him a sad look, then hugged him again. This hug was for Dannol, but Beol didn't begrudge him one bit.

"He's badly shaken. No one's angry at him, but he feels so guilty. He's been working tirelessly to help clean up," Beol said.

"He needs rest, just like anyone else," Meggie said. "You need rest too, kitty. Beck's patched up and in bed. Nettle needed the space in the Med Bay. He's on bedrest for at least a few days."

"Bloop's with him?"

"Of course."

Beol went to their bedroom and stood in the doorway, smiling. Beck was sprawled across the bed, leg wrapped up tight. Dr. Bloop lay stretched out, snuggled against his side with his head on Beck's shoulder.

Beol sat at the corner desk and called Bendix. He might as well check in one more time before giving in to sleep.

"Hey, boss man," Bendix said. Beol could hear talking and could see several people moving behind Bendix. "We got your report earlier. We're throwing a wake now for Clara, Jossa, and Derran. Beck's parents and sisters are here too."

"Did Fasi and the Council decide yet?"

"Fasi's making the call tomorrow morning. He wanted to give you all time to recuperate, but yeah. The Bracken are full citizens of Charybdis Station, and the Fyrlings are a protected animal species."

Beol breathed out, relieved. That was one less thing to worry about.

"That's not all though," Bendix said. "Believe it or not, that reporter's footage of Sax, Icarus, and Meggie impressed a lot of people. Two other planets offered them recognition as a sentient species and citizenship."

"What footage? I didn't think Jen had released anything yet."

"She released the first one right after the battle. It was a lot of interviews with the Bracken, the Charybdis Station crews, and the former prisoners on Genarg. She even talked to Leti and Sebastian. There was one interview with Clara that about breaks my heart."

Beol closed his eyes, heart aching. "There's more?"

"The second one came out a few hours ago. It was Remy's rite of passage and a bunch of other interviews as you all prepared for the Queen. It had a really sweet conversation with Meggie and Dannol."

"She didn't interview me," Beol said, opening his eyes again.

"You're not exactly sweet." Bendix shrugged. "She did get video of you and Beck cuddling though. Anyway, the last one was of the battle. The media released it an hour ago."

"All that helped the Bracken?"

"Hell yeah. They have fan clubs now." Bendix

rubbed his hands over his face. "That was some crazy shit."

"It could have gone a lot worse."

"Don't we always say that when we survive? No matter the loss, it could have been worse."

"Beol!" Hay's face appeared over Bendix's shoulder. "Why aren't you asleep? The babies need rest."

Beol smiled softly at his friend. "That is a very good point. These babies say it's time to steal some of the bed from my mate."

Bendix and Hay grinned. "Oh, and boss man. The Council voted on one more thing after seeing that footage."

"What?"

"You're now the Full-Moon General of Charybdis Station."

21

ONE MONTH LATER

$\mathcal{B}$eck held Beol's hand as they walked down the main street in the newly named town of Dragon's Hollow. Bloop loped beside them, still puppyish even though he was huge.

Beck looked up. Okay, so he had to admit, Princess Buttercup was an inspiring sight to see as he flew over the town, Leti and Hack on his back. Dragon's Hollow was a good name.

"They're going to do this all the time when we get back to the station, aren't they?" Beol smiled as he watched them slowly circle the town.

"The Lord Admiral isn't gonna be impressed," Beck said and grinned.

Repairs to the city were coming along well, and Alber and Beck had managed to repair the planetary defenses. Just in time too. They had already received merchant ships, eager to develop a trading route with Genarg.

"Do you think Earth will take the contract for

Union Station?" Beol sounded wistful. "Imagine the planet whole and fresh again."

Representatives from Union Station had approached Earth about healing their planet. The surface was in ruins, but the planet itself wasn't completely unlivable like Genarg had been. Sebastian had said it wouldn't take her nearly the amount of time to heal it as it had taken her to heal Genarg.

"I think she will. Once the babies are born," Beck said. "She may just train someone to do it too. She seemed sympathetic, and they offered a shit ton of credits."

"It's strange, but I'm actually going to miss this place," Beol said. "Don't get me wrong; I want to get home ASAP. Bendix has approved Full-Moon's uniforms, and I don't trust him."

Hack and his small fleet had stayed on the planet to repair their ships and let the injured heal.

"We leave tomorrow," Beck said, squeezing his hand. "We'll be home in a month and a half."

Beck tried to ignore the pang he felt at leaving one particular little pile of dirt.

"What's wrong, Sparky?"

"How do you do that?" Beck pouted. His mate could read him like a book.

"It's not hard," Beol said, voice full of amusement. "Now, answer the question."

Beck bit his lip. "I don't want to leave the baby."

"The one you and Bloop curl around every day?"

The one I caught Beol visiting too, Beck thought.

"Yeah. I don't know why I'm so drawn to the little girl, but I am."

"The babies still have a week before they're born."

"I know," Beck said, trying not to think about it. "We'll be long gone by then."

Beol stopped walking abruptly and leaned up to kiss Beck. "Hmm. I need to check in with Noe and see how he's doing."

Beol pulled away and hustled toward the temple where Sebastian and the others tended to gather. The gold throne had been melted down and now the large room was an airy training ground for the shamans.

"I'm not the only obvious one, Beol," Beck called out. He looked at Bloop. "Well, what do you say we go check on the baby?"

"Woof."

"Good call."

Beck slipped into the jungle and undressed before shifting. He lifted his nose in the air and enjoyed the jungle's unique scent, his tag wagging. Bloop licked his ear, and the two took off toward the Hollow.

He passed Icarus and Juniper along the way. The two were working with Remy and Ninetta in the vegetable garden. Without the threat of the Queen hanging over their heads, the new citizens of Genarg were expanding their gardens and settling in. Icarus and Juniper were having the time of their lives designing the perfect farms around the town.

Remy and Jalyn had both decided to stay on Genarg instead of going back to Charybdis Station. They felt a connection to the planet and wanted to continue protecting it and training shamans.

They weren't the only ones who had decided to stay. Many of the human rebels from Vextonar refused to go back there. They had settled in well and were helping to rebuild the city.

That was good and all, but no one had been exactly happy when Haroon and two of his crew decided to stay as well. Haroon didn't have anything waiting on him back at the station and wanted a fresh start. They had all held their tongues, knowing the widower needed to get away.

Hack had flat-out thrown a fit though, when Xav had insisted on staying too, at least temporarily. A few of his crew would join him.

When Xav wouldn't listen to him, Hack had called his parents. Fasi and Renee Juren had surprised everyone when they had been completely supportive and practically glowed with pride over Xav's decision.

Beck stopped for a moment. Potato lounged at the edge of the garden, enjoying the sun. Beck leaned over and licked the cat's head and was rewarded with a hiss.

"Leave my cat alone, Beck," Remy said, laughing. "I swear you look all wolfish, but you're a big puppy."

Beck barked a goodbye and headed farther toward the jungle. He noticed Morgan at the graveyard again. Wyatt sat with him in front of Hazel's grave. She had no family, so they had decided to bury her here with Beol's people.

Beck padded over and settled his head on Morgan's

shoulder. He whined, and Morgan lifted a hand and pet him.

"I'm okay, Beck. We lose people sometimes, and it's hard. I trained her and spent a lot of time with her. I'm going to miss her."

Bloop licked Morgan's cheek, and the man laughed.

"Hey now, Dr. Bloop," Wyatt said. "That's my man."

Beck and Bloop left them to their peace and contemplation and went into the jungle. Soon enough, they came across another couple. For such a small planet, it sure was crowded.

Meggie and Dannol sat on a blanket in a small clearing. Meggie was mostly functional again, but she still had no outer flesh, skin, or hair. Becca and Gregor were working on it back at Charybdis, but Beck simply didn't have the materials.

Dannol didn't seem to care as he laughed at a story she was telling about Rus and his first kiss with Sax.

Beck paused beside them and pinned Meggie down to lick her metal face. Bloop joined in.

"Eww! You two are disgusting." She pushed them away. "Go visit your baby"

Beck barked, then got back to running. He only stopped three more times to sniff things with Bloop.

Earth, Death, and Fire were already at the Hollow. Fire's guinea pigs sat on his shoulders.

"Come to see your girl?" Earth arched a brow.

Bloop stopped to say hello to the Elements and to get his ears scratched, while Beck slid into the pit and went straight to the pile of dirt that held his baby Crell.

He didn't understand why he was drawn to her,

but it broke his heart to leave her. He loved her as much as he loved the twins growing in Beol's belly and Icarus.

He whined and lay his head on his paws.

Earth sat beside him in the dirt and settled her hand on his head. "This one is yours, isn't she?"

Beck woofed softly.

"I never thought I would be so happy without my Queen with me," Earth said. "I miss her, but rebuilding Genarg and bringing back the Crell are accomplishments she would be proud of." Earth scratched his ears. "I never intended any of these children to leave Genarg, but this little girl truly is yours. Would you care for her, Beck, as you care for your Icarus? As you will soon care for your twins?"

Beck sat up and shifted, unconcerned with his nakedness. "Seriously, Earth? I could adopt her?"

Earth's eyes softened. "I think you and Beol would be the perfect parents for her."

Beck swallowed, sadness filling him. "We're leaving tomorrow."

Hack groaned as he sat beside Beck, startling him. "We're leaving after your baby is born, Beckie Boo."

Beck's eyes grew wide, and he grabbed his tail, grinning from ear to ear. "Really?"

Selene sat gracefully next to Hack. "Your mate told us about the baby. Why didn't you say anything?"

Beck looked around. "Where's Beol?"

"He's six months pregnant," Hack said dryly. "The man's slow."

"You left him in the jungle alone?" Beck growled.

"No, I left him with Leti and Princess. Plus, there are no animals on the planet. Don't worry."

"He is an assassin, Beck," Selene reminded him.

The bigger Beol's belly got, the easier it was to forget.

"We told everyone why we were delaying, and they're all for it," Hack said, then looked at the pile of dirt. "So, this is your kid, huh?"

Earth hummed sweetly and smiled. "You won't have to delay your departure."

The dirt slid away with a wave of her hand. The child inside moved around, and the translucent sack shuddered.

"That sack thing looks like it's about to take a shit," Hack said.

"Don't speak, Hack. You'll ruin the moment," Selene said.

Beck grimaced but didn't turn away. It really did look like it was about to shit.

"What's happening?" Beol called out from the top of the small pit. "Why didn't you put clothes on, Sparky? We store them here for a reason."

"The baby's coming, Beol." Beck jumped up and climbed up the side of the pit to pick up his mate and carry him back to the baby.

"Fuck, that looks disgusting."

"Welcome to the joys of childbirth," Leti said as he slid down. "I'll let everyone know she's coming."

After a few hours of straining, the baby slipped out of the sack. Beck was there to catch her, tears in his eyes. Beol stood right beside him, eyes watering too.

Meggie, Nettle, Wyatt, and Rune shuffled around, each one trying to get a look at the baby. Meggie's scanner worked, even if her injectors were out of commission for a while.

She scanned the baby and showed the results to Nettle. "She's so beautiful, Beck."

"She's healthy too."

Wyatt carefully washed her off with water, then handed her to Rune to swaddle.

Leti snickered. "Two doctors and two medics here to deliver a baby from a planet."

"Yeah, we weren't needed," Nettle said, shrugging. "She's the first Crell born in centuries."

"What's her name, Beck?" Hack sat with Leti in his lap.

"I'm no good with names," he said shaking his head. "Beol, what do you think?"

"What about Aketil? I've always liked that name."

"Oh, I like it," Icarus said. He and Sax sat close by as he waited to see his little sister.

Beck grinned. "It's perfect. She's perfect."

Rune settled the baby into Beck's arms. Beck felt like his heart would burst from his chest and do cartwheels across the jungle.

Aketil was a newborn, but she was big. Beck remembered the pictures Leti had shown them. The Crell were huge, easily towering over even the Grell and Betonize. She had soft green skin and a tuft of white hair on her head. Two tiny tusks framed her little mouth.

Her dark eyes stared straight up at Beck, and he fell

hard. He remembered feeling this same way when Icarus awoke for the first time. He knew he'd feel it again when Beol had the twins.

Earth closed her eyes and hummed, sounding suspiciously like Mustachio. She glowed with a dark green light.

They all watched in awe as the sack shuddered and closed again. The dirt underneath it shifted, and a small embryo nestled into the sack.

She waved her hand, and soil covered it again. It would take centuries, but the Crells would live again.

*B*eol held Aketil in his arms as they all gathered in the conference room on the Blue Solace. They were only a few weeks away from Charybdis Station, but they had to go to Derelict for fuel, instead of Vextonar for obvious reasons.

Fasi's purple face filled the screen, looking far too calm for the news he'd just given them.

"A large HF fleet is headed toward Charybdis Station?" Hack was pale. "Why are you smiling, Dad?"

"We have it handled son. You all may get back in time to help, but Draif has it covered."

"If Otto's numbers are correct, our Fleet is evenly matched with theirs. That is no reason not to worry." Selene tilted her head. "You have something up your sleeve."

Beol grinned when Fasi laughed. "That we do, Selene darling. That we do."

The Blue Solace Series – science fiction/fantasy, mpreg

1. The Mercenary's Mate – https://amzn.to/2MAOFEH
2. The General's Mate – https://amzn.to/2G1abRE
3. The Soldier's Mate – https://amzn.to/2S7R6ng
4. The Lieutenant's Mate – https://amzn.to/2THZ47w
5. The Engineer's Mate – https://amzn.to/2HpI4vH
6. The Captain's Mate – https://amzn.to/2knP03W
7. The Rebel's Mate – *Coming Soon*

*More sci-fi spin-off series from the Blue Solace book world
will be coming soon.

The Hobson Hills Omegas – non-shifter, mpreg,
omegaverse

1. Falling for the Omega – https://amzn.to/2BgWURV
2. Snow Kisses for My Omega – https://amzn.to/2TdDiol
3. Romancing the Omega – https://

amzn.to/2UNENKD

4. Healing the Omega – https://
    amzn.to/2FNcXrY

5. A Pint for my Omega – https://
    amzn.to/2XItQf7

6. Unraveling the Omega – https://
    amzn.to/2xRCnRL

7. The Alpha's Christmas Wish – https://
    amzn.to/2qXkGAl

8. Noah's story (Title to be determined) –
    Coming Soon

Hobson Hills Shorts – short stories from the world of
Hobson Hills Omegas

1. The Beta's Love Song – https://
    amzn.to/2UrRPNN

2. Bennett's Dream – https://
    amzn.to/2GwSpG3

3. Justin's Journey – https://amzn.to/2DhW1t1

4. Grey's Gift – https://amzn.to/2BcjxXf

5. Hobson Hills Shorts: Volume One – https://
    amzn.to/2M3oGGZ

Holiday Omegas Shorts – holiday short stories from the
world of The Silver Isles – paranormal, mpreg

1. Cauldron Cake Pops and a Witch's Kiss –
    https://amzn.to/33wMrhc

2. Sugar Cookies and a Witch's Love – https://
    amzn.to/2NE4CeJ

3. Candy Hearts and a Witch's Ring – *Coming in February, 2020*

The Silver Isles – paranormal, mermen, mpreg

1. The Guppy Prince – https://amzn.to/2q9Q8en
2. The Not so Little Merman – *Coming Soon*
3. The Sea Witch – *Coming Soon*

If you would like to keep up with releases, please like and follow me on Instagram (@c.w._gray) or Facebook (@cwgrayauthor), join C.W. Gray's Reading Nook on Facebook, or visit my website at cwgray.com

EXCERPT

Excerpt from *The Captain's Mate* – book six in The Blue Solace

Anchors Rest System, Charybdis Station

"Dottie, I can't thank you enough for your contact list," Draif Ando said, smiling at the older woman on the screen in front of him. Her wild and tangled grey hair stuck up in all directions from the wind that blew through the spaceport on Vextonar.

Dottie was a bit crazy and a bit evil mastermind, but she had a heart as big as the galaxy, and had been one of the few to really *see* him when they lived on Vextonar. There had been more than a few times, her strong arms had held him as he cried. Her strange mixed-up scent of ship fumes and basil was as familiar to him as the scars on his face.

Draif cleared his throat, chasing away the nostalgia. "Each person you introduced me to has been helpful in hunting down the information I need. A few even sent me on to some of their own contacts."

Dottie's wide grin lit up her eyes. "Good. It took me years to find them, but they're good and talented folks. I know you'll treat them right."

Draif grinned. "They like my money just as much as yours. I'm putting my pieces in place, and we'll catch Humans First unawares."

Her body shook with her laugh. "I knew the first time we met that you were a sneaky bastard, kiddo. You remind me of an Old-Earth bird I read about. Black Herons would hunt fish in the shallows by spreading their wings over one spot and tricking the fish into thinking it was night. The poor fish would poke their heads up, believing they were safe and the Black Heron would eat them up."

"I'll do my best to take HF down," Draif said, nodding. "They're arrogant fuckers. I don't think they understand what they're getting into."

Dottie looked sad for a moment. "It's getting bad here, kiddo. Vextonar has always been specieist, but the government and the Prime are pushing harder and harder each day. They want a planet of pure-blooded humans."

Draif frowned. "There are no pureblood humans anymore. Besides, the Prime like their slaves and servants. How does that fit?"

She shrugged. "I didn't say they were making sense, Draify. I think that's what scares me the most. It's like something is stirring the pot just to see it boil over."

"It has to be Humans First. We'll deal with it."

Dottie smiled softly. "You're a good boy, Draif. Did you know that Lord Admiral of yours personally called me up to thank me for sending you and Leti to them?"

Draif scratched his ear. "Oh, well, Fasi loves Leti. He's married to Fasi's son, after all."

She arched a brow. "We all love Leti, Draif, but we love you too. You're a good addition to the Station and Lord Admiral Juren knows it. Don't sell yourself short, kiddo."

Draif didn't know how to respond. He knew people put up with him for Leti's sake, and he tried to be as helpful as possible, but love was a completely different thing.

A beeping sound came through from Dottie's end, and she groaned. "Okay. Our secure line is breaking. Take care, kiddo. Give them hell."

Buy Here: https://amzn.to/2knP03W

Excerpt from *Falling for the Omega*– Book One in the Hobson Hills Omegas Series

Carter loaded the last of his tools into his new work van and shut the door. His first day in his new profession was off to a good start. He had three clients to see today and eight spread out during the rest of the week.

Finally getting his plumbing license had been a good idea, even if his perfect, wealthy family hated the idea of him being a plumber.

Hell, they had also hated the idea of him being a soldier and of him moving out of state when he came back injured. They pretty much hated every decision he made.

The crisp fall wind was cold, but the gold, brown, and red leaves on the trees and ground made the cold worth dealing with. Autumn in Maine sure wasn't the same as autumn in Georgia, but so far, he was damn happy with the move. There was a peace here amongst the trees that he hadn't managed to find anywhere else.

"Hi, Mr. Neighbor!"

A child's voice came from behind him, startling Carter. He spun around, stumbling a bit on his prosthesis, and faced the little girl standing a few feet from his van.

She looked about five or six, with two black braids, caramel skin, and a freckled nose. When she smiled brightly, he saw a small gap between her two front teeth.

A black and gray miniature schnauzer sat at her feet, gaze stern and trained on him.

He looked around and didn't see any adults. His little half acre tract was quite a ways back from the road, nestled between a good-sized apple orchard on one side and a thick forest on the other.

Where the hell had this little girl come from?

"My name's Olive, and I brought you a welcome basket. I made it myself, but Daddy made you one too. He's gonna bring it tonight. I wanted you to get mine first, 'cause it's from me and then we'll be best friends." The little girl paused to take a breath. Her wide brown eyes sparkled and met his straight on, innocent and fearless. "We'll be best friends forever."

She didn't even seem to see the scars along the side of his face. The burn marks had already made two kids cry at the grocery store yesterday. Both times, the parents had been too embarrassed to apologize. They just grabbed their kids and ran.

"Uh, where's your daddy, Olive?" His voice was

deep and cracked, broken by the scarring on his neck. Her adoring stare was starting to freak him out a little. He'd never really been around kids.

"He's at home," she answered and handed him the basket. "See what I brought you? Look, look, look."

"Do you know your phone number? Maybe we could give your daddy a call," Carter said, taking the basket from Olive. He pulled the small hand towel from the top and almost dropped the basket. "Is that a hedgehog?"

"Yep! That's Hodges the hedgehog. He wanted to come visit too. Oh and this is Winston," she said and knelt to pet the small dog.

"Okay, your number?" He tried to keep his gruff voice kind. No sense in scaring the kid.

"Olive! Olive Persephone Wilson! Where are you?" A man's voice called from the orchard, full of panic and desperation.

"Uh oh," Olive said. She hurriedly looked around, then darted behind his van, Winston following her. "That's Daddy." She poked her head out and stared hard. "Tell. Him. Nothing."

She quickly hid again when a young omega rushed out of the orchard. He was her father, had to be. He looked just like her.

Carter suddenly couldn't catch his breath. The man in front of him was simply adorable. He was short and well formed, a little chubby. His black hair fell in curls around his face, and his wide hazel eyes contrasted beautifully with his caramel skin. The same freckles that decorated his daughter's nose, fell across his own.

Where it looked cute on the kid, on her father... Bad thoughts, Carter! Bad thoughts!

"Have you seen a little girl? Black hair? Brown eyes? Miniature schnauzer with her? Maybe a hedgehog?"

Carter stared at the handsome man, mouth gaping, for too long.

The man frowned at him, tilting his head. "Are you alright?" His shy smile revealed the small gap between his front teeth.

Oh fuck, he was so damn perfect. He met Carter's eyes too, didn't even glance at the scars.

"Mister?"

Carter shook his head and did his best to pull himself together. He smiled, as best he could with the scar tissue, and nodded toward the van, holding a finger to his lips, encouraging the man to keep quiet.

Olive's father rolled his eyes and stomped around the van. A squealing Olive ran from her hiding spot and hid behind Carter, hugging him around the waist.

"Mr. Neighbor, save me!" Her giggling told him she wasn't too worried about her father catching her.

"Olive, you scared me to death running off like that." Her father really did look worried. "What have I told you about leaving the house without me?"

"But daddy," she whined. "I wanted to meet Mr. Neighbor. We're best friends now, and I gave him a welcome basket. I was being hospital."

Carter frowned. Hospital?

"Hospitable, baby girl, and it doesn't matter. You are too little to be wandering around by yourself and talking to strangers. No television time this week, and you have to clean out Pooka and Banjo's stalls on Saturday."

Olive gave a big sigh and leaned her forehead into Carter's leg. "Okay, Daddy, but it was worth it. I have a new best friend now."

The man met Carter's stare, a question in his eyes. Carter nodded and gave his best half smile.

"Well, maybe our new neighbor would like to come over for dinner one night? So that we can meet him properly," the man said.

"Yay! Mr. Neighbor, can you come tonight? Daddy's gonna make apple dumplins for dessert."

Carter smiled at the little girl and nodded. "Yeah, if it's okay with your dad."

The man smiled and nodded eagerly. "That would be great. I hardly ever get to cook for anyone but Olive." He gave a flustered look and held out his hand. "Oh, I forgot. My name is Elijah Wilson. I live in the farmhouse with the orchard. Of course, you've met Olive."

Carter shook his hand, touch lingering longer than it should. He was reluctant to release him but finally did. "Yeah, I'm Carter Benson. Just moved here from Georgia."

"Wow, so Maine's probably a bit different, huh?"

"Yeah, but all the colors on the trees? And ya'll actually have snow. I've never seen much of it."

"You say that like snow is a good thing." Elijah shuddered. "Well, welcome to Hobson Hill. I see Olive already gave you a welcome basket."

Carter looked back in it. "There's a hedgehog in

there." His coarse voice was getting rougher as he spoke. He wasn't used to talking so much. Doctors said it was good for him to do though.

"I put cider in there for you. It's in my favorite big girl cup, the one with Moana. There's also butter from Pooka and some of Daddy's bread. It's so yummy!"

"Thanks, Olive. I appreciate it," Carter said. The little girl still hung on his leg, smiling up at him. She was a cute one, he acknowledged, even though she was clearly a little crazy. It was a good crazy though.

"Your alpha won't mind me coming," Carter asked Elijah.

The man winced and lowered his eyes. "I don't have an Alpha, so no, that won't be a problem."

Carter was surprised. Happy, but surprised. This adorable man had to be beating them off with a stick. Of course, some folks thought poorly about single omegas, and some alphas refused to even speak to them. Idiots.

"I guess I'll see you tonight. What time?"

"Oh, is six okay?" Elijah's confidence seemed to bounce back at Carter's question.

"That's fine. I better get to work."

"Yes, of course," Elijah said and pulled Olive off Carter's leg. "Come on, Olive. We better get back to the house. We need to get you to school."

"Okay. Bye, Carter, love you!" The little girl and her dog ran off through the orchard.

"I swear it's exhausting keeping up with her," Elijah sighed. Carter smiled and held the hedgehog out to him. "Thanks," he said, taking Hodges and smiling shyly. "See you tonight. Have a good day at work."

Carter stood frozen as he watched Elijah walk away. He was in trouble. Big, wonderful trouble.

Buy Here: My Book

EXCERPT

Excerpt from *The Guppy Prince*, book one in The Silver Isles.

Dover Rees floated in the deepest part of his creek, enjoying the rushing sound of the waterfall to his right. Sunlight filtered through the water, glinting off the deep blue of his guppy tail. His thin and delicate caudal fin spread out like an elegant fan, dancing through the warm water as he swayed.

His favorite smooth and colorful pebbles were strewn around below him, and he admired the shells he had collected and placed beside them. Dover breathed deeply and enjoyed the peace and quiet. No one mocked him or bossed him around. No one watched him with cold eyes and hidden smirks. *I wish I could stay here forever.*

Sudden movement beside him jarred him from his thoughts and he laughed when Chubber grabbed a bright pink stone in his small brown paws and swam away. Dover's otter friend liked to steal Dover's shinies then share them with him again later.

A brook trout swam past him and Dover debated grabbing it for an early lunch, but he wasn't too hungry yet. Lately, he'd been eating less and less, and he couldn't make himself care.

The quiet water around him hummed as Nami quickly swam to him. His best friend's guppy tail was a lovely pink pattern with black dots, and her short black hair floated around her head. The cat with a mermaid tail on her black tankini top made him smile. He loved her purr-maid shirts.

"Have you eaten today, Your Highness?" she asked.

Dover scowled. "Don't call me that."

"When you're acting like a pouting asswipe, that's what you get called." Nami wrapped her arms around him and settled her head on his shoulder. "What's wrong with you, Dover?"

Dover had no answer for her. All he knew was he felt empty inside and it was harder and harder to get up in the morning. "I think I ate some bad clams."

"Every day for the past two months?" Nami leaned back and glared at him, her dark eyes seeing right through him.

Chubber came to his rescue, swimming in between them and wrapping his lean body across Dover's shoulders. "Chubber wants to get a snack."

Nami sighed, bubbles filling the water around her. "Mom is in your cottage making lunch. You're worrying us, bluetail."

Dover stroked a hand through her hair, then shoved

her down and pushed up, swimming toward the surface.

"Damn it!" Nami swam after him.

He laughed, heart warming. *Someone cares about me.* It wasn't his family, but Nami and her mom were closer to him than his parents or any of his twelve siblings.

Chubber clung to his back and nibbled on his ear until he mentally apologized. Chubber cared about him the most.

His creek was deep, but it didn't take him long to reach the surface. Shauna waited for them on the shore, hands on her hips. Chubber's mother, Shell, stood on her hind legs beside the mermaid, chirping loudly. Uh oh. He really was in trouble.

"You didn't eat breakfast, did you?" The wind blew strands of Shauna's pink hair across her face, ruining her glare.

"Sorry, Shauna."

She sighed. "I made your favorite."

"Grilled shrimp salad?" Dover's stomach rumbled.

"With avocado, papaya, mango, and pineapple. All your favorites." Shauna gave him a soft look. "Come eat, bluetail."

Dover summoned his human legs and a few seconds later, walked out of the creek, naked, with Chubber clinging to his shoulder. Shauna handed him a deep teal sarong, and he tied it about his waist.

Shell crawled up his leg and into his arms, then rubbed her slick furry face against his. She was a bit heavier than Chubber, but he was still a baby.

"Why does he get all the loving?" Nami asked, grumbling as she tied a sarong around her own waist.

Dover chuckled when Shauna arched an eyebrow at her daughter. "Did you say something, sweetness?"

"No, ma'am," Nami said, wincing.

"You two come eat lunch." Shauna turned around and walked toward Dover's large cottage.

Dover closed his eyes for a moment and savored the feel of the moss-covered rocks under his feet, and the comfortable breeze quickly drying his curly blue hair. He loved his home so much. It was his sanctuary.

Buy Here: https://amzn.to/2q9Q8en